ADVANCE PRAISE FOR
THE SECRETEST OF SECRETISMS

'The best book ever written'
God, author of the Bible

'Unfortunately, I passed away before the publication of *The Secretest of Secretisms*. However, I was brought back to life by God in order to read it. "Get a load of this, Tolstoy, it's bonza – it absolutely shits on *War and Peace*!" he said. And I've got to say, he wasn't lying. What a heart-stopping thrill ride!'
Leo Tolstoy

'Yup, got to agree with Tolstoy there. The boy's hit the nail on the head. Absolutely corking stuff. I am sincerely jealous and wish I could write as well as Dave Beige'
William Shakespeare

'Far better than anything I achieved in my ninety years of life'
Winston Churchill

'I came, I devoured, I adored'
Julius Caesar

'Makes other authors feel inadequate. Beige is the new Black!'
Charles Dickens

'That Tolstoy speaks good English, don't he?'
Winston Churchill

'That he does. Nice beard too'
William Shakespeare

'Oi, Shakespeare! Did I just see that you wrote a play about me? It better be about my military victories and genius as a tactician or you can bloody step outside, mate!'
Julius Caesar

'Right, come on lads, let's get a quick one down the Coach and Horses before God sends us back. Your round, Churchill, and you can put some of that insurance money to good use'
Charles Dickens

'Ohhhh yes'
Winston Churchill

THE SECRETEST OF SECRETISMS
A PARODY

DAVE BEIGE

WITH BRUNO VINCENT

THE SECRETEST OF SECRETISMS

A PARODY

HarperCollins*Publishers*

For Brig with Love

HarperCollins*Publishers*
1 London Bridge Street
London SE1 9GF

www.harpercollins.co.uk

HarperCollins*Publishers*
Macken House, 39/40 Mayor Street Upper
Dublin 1, D01 C9W8, Ireland

First published by HarperCollins*Publishers* 2025

1 3 5 7 9 10 8 6 4 2

© Bruno Vincent 2025

Bruno Vincent asserts the moral right to
be identified as the author of this work

A catalogue record of this book is
available from the British Library

ISBN 978-0-00-878313-6

Printed and bound in the UK using 100 per cent
renewable electricity at CPI Group (UK) Ltd

All rights reserved. No part of this publication may be
reproduced, stored in a retrieval system, or transmitted,
in any form or by any means, electronic, mechanical,
photocopying, recording or otherwise, without the
prior written permission of the publishers.

Without limiting the author's and publisher's exclusive
rights, any unauthorised use of this publication to train
generative artificial intelligence (AI) technologies is expressly
prohibited. HarperCollins also exercise their rights under
Article 4(3) of the Digital Single Market Directive 2019/790
and expressly reserve this publication from the text and
data mining exception.

This book contains FSC™ certified paper and other controlled
sources to ensure responsible forest management.

For more information visit: www.harpercollins.co.uk/green

PROLOGUE

The windows were covered with black cloth to keep out the beating sun, and to create a private sanctum within the hushed stone dwelling.

This stone house, fashioned from the local rock by the hands of humble peasants, was itself a secret, known only to a few. It nurtured secrets within its very depths, within the hearts and minds of the people who had come here. Within the occult rites, too, which they were about to perform. Secrecy lay within its every stone and permeated its fibre, like the mint flavouring in mint ice cream.

A chamber of secrets, one might say, if that phrase wasn't already taken.

Above the door, a handful of words were carved into the lintel in an ancient local dialect.

It communicated a dire warning. A curse.

A man came to the door, cloaked head to toe in a secretive cloak. He looked up and read those words. Roughly translated, they read:

Mind your own bloody business, mate.

Absolute silence prevailed in the searing afternoon heat, broken only by the occasional cricket, the screech of a mountain eagle, someone in a neighbouring garden mowing the lawn and listening to the radio, and the recently completed motorway bypass.

The man looked over his shoulder, unsure if he was the last to arrive.

'Come on, everyone!' he shouted. 'It's nearly time for the secret ceremony no one's supposed to know about!'

'Ssshhh!' whispered a voice. A hand came out of the darkness, grabbed him and yanked him inwards.

Inside, several cloaked individuals were gathered around the table in the centre of the room. It was lit by four candles.

Fork handles in hands, they raised their fists in salute as the secret ceremony they were performing reached its climax.

'Bow to the saint, Alphonso,' said the one leading the ceremony, gesturing to a painting on the table.

An enormous figure to his right bowed. The others were covered in cloaks, but it had not been possible to find one suitably massive enough to cloak the initiate. Therefore his cloak had been improvised from a horse blanket.

'Not to me, Alphonso. To the saint. To the picture. Here.'

It appeared that the enormous figure had got his cloak twisted round and couldn't see, for he bumbled while trying to see where was being indicated.

'That's it,' said the master of ceremonies, after quite a long delay. He let out a relieved sigh. 'Now, Alphonso. Do you promise your life to our cause?'

'Um, yeah,' said a muffled voice from beneath the horse blanket.

'Just say, "I promise,"' said the other. 'Now, do you promise to serve us and follow all our orders, on pain of death?'

'I guess,' said the muffled voice.

'Just say, "I promise,"' muttered the other, icily. One of his confrères leaned in and whispered, 'Forgeddabout it, just let him do it his way.'

'And you promise to stay loyal to this secret fraternity for the rest of your days, and to have loyalty to us only and to no other person or group, religion, leader or monarch upon this earth?'

'Sure,' said the muffled voice.

'It wouldn't goddam kill him just to say, "I friggin' promise," is my point,' the master of ceremonies whispered viciously, to nobody in particular.

Then more loudly, he went on: 'I will now prick your finger so we can seal this agreement by your signing in your own blood.'

'Ow, hurts,' said the voice plaintively from under the horse blanket.

'Just sign here,' said the Exasperated One. 'Initial here and here, and date it here. Oh, sweet Jesus …'

And to bring an end to the bumbling, he took the hand and splodged blood on the document that was laid out for signature: once, twice, thrice.

'So it is signed this day in full view of the Holy Saint, meaning that you, Alphonso Emmettio, are a brother of our Secret Society.'

The other men all clapped him heartily on the back and uttered words of congratulation.

'This is a sacred ceremony and eternally binding,' said the Master of Ceremonies grandly. 'By so signing, you have signed away your soul. And now – nibbles.'

'Ooo, nibbles,' said the enormous figure, who had been sucking his pricked finger and showing little attention to the preceding speech.

The ceremony completed to the satisfaction of all, the need for secrecy was no more. The horse blanket was thus removed, albeit the figure presently revealed did not show a great deal more animation than when the blanket had been in place. Of course, the windows were still covered and it was hard for anyone in the room to make him out.

But he gave off the impression of a kind of lopsided doughy mountain more than a man, with a curious absent expression rather as though on pause while downloading an important update.

Still, everyone likes nibbles. And thus Alphonso was roused to as close to actual animation as he ever got, scooping whole bowlfuls of crunchy snacks into his cavernous mouth. Meanwhile others stood by and sipped red wine circumspectly, glancing at his enormous bulk.

'Me go now,' said the man-mountain presently. And lumbering to the door, he wandered out into the Sicilian sunshine and away down the rough mountain track.

Two sagacious-looking men came to stand in the doorway and watch him depart.

'Have we made a correct decision, do you think?' asked one. 'What we need him to do is no easy task.'

'He came very highly recommended,' said the other. 'We have given him his instructions.'

They both watched as the figure tripped and stumbled slightly over a stone on the path.

'All our hopes rest on him,' said the first.

As they watched, Alphonso, now a hundred yards away, jumped in terror at something to the side of the path and sprinted away with thunderous footsteps. Behind him, from within a bush, a chicken wandered onto the track. It too watched him retreat.

The two men's attention was now arrested by someone else, coming down the mountain from the other direction. This was a fine figure of a young man: muscular, athletic and handsome.

'My friends!' he gasped, coming to a stop. 'I'm here!'

The elderly gentlemen regarded the stranger coldly.

'Forgive me for being late to my own initiation ceremony,' the young man said. 'I was given the wrong address by my idiot cousin, Alphonso. My god, that guy is such an imbecile. If he concentrated hard for an hour, perhaps he might work out how to pick his nose.'

His two interlocutors exchanged a dark and meaningful look.

'Sometimes we feel it would be best for the family if he just fell down a well and drowned. What a *mook*, a *babbo*. But, brothers, I am here – Alonso. I'm honoured to be inducted into your fraternity ...'

'You cannot speak this way about a Made Man,' said the elder of the two gents.

'This is a very serious crime against us,' said the other.

The young man laughed – then saw they were in earnest. 'But ... a Made Man? You cannot be serious ...'

'Take this youth round the back and shoot him,' said the elder of the two. 'As a lesson to others.'

'At once,' said the other, gesturing to two accomplices who had emerged from the darkness of the room behind.

'It will be done.'

1

Respected Harvard Professor Richard Wangley, world expert in Secretistical Symboligism, gripped the arms of his chair.

His pulse raced and it felt as though his heart would burst from his chest.

Sweat streamed from his forehead.

Pinned to his seat, he thrashed left, then right.

'My god!' he gasped.

His eyes opened and he stared about him with desperation.

'Are you okay?' said the woman in the seat beside him. She leaned forward with concern and placed a placatory hand on his forearm. She was beautiful, with long hazel locks and lavish eyelashes that were – however – hidden behind decidedly sober and business-like spectacles. She had chosen them very deliberately as in her experience, good looks could be a severe impediment to career advancement in the heavily male-influenced world she had chosen to work in. In this case, the world of experimental science.

'Darling,' she added, and her eyes flashed with fondness. It was instantly clear that between the world-renowned

Scientific Symbolist and his as-yet-relatively-unknown-but-soon-to-be-very-well-known-indeed-neighbour, Susannah Moses, there was more than mere professional esteem.

'I was having a dreadful nightmare!' said Wangley, his voice shaking. He wiped his forehead with his handkerchief and waited for his pulse to steady.

'Tell me about it,' cooed his feminine but at the same time highly dignified and independent inamorata, with a concerned frown.

'It was horrible,' Wangley said, looking distraught. 'I was in a historical capital city, and after the hideous murder of a respected cultural official, I had to go on the run with a talented but damaged young woman and solve a sequence of clues, while being simultaneously chased by law enforcement and a grotesquely physically hideous murderer, who was hell-bent on the revelation (or suppression, in the dream it wasn't quite clear) of a world-changing secret!'

'How horrible for you,' murmured his girlfriend, in tones that were somehow loving and sensual, without compromising any of her autonomy as a person, which he respected even more deeply as a consequence. 'You were reliving that horrible experience you had in Paris a few years ago, no doubt, when you were mixed up in the search for the Holy Grail …'

'No, it wasn't that,' Wangley insisted, his eyes misty as he probed the dream for details.

'It must have been the time you went on the run in Bilbao then, after an assassination at the Guggenheim Museum, which was intended to cover up the secret truth behind the Creation of Life on Earth?'

'It wasn't that either,' said Wangley unhappily, squirming in his seat.

'Ah,' said Susannah, 'of course – it must refer to the time you had to escape armed police and solve the murders of four cardinals in Rome, in order to prevent the Vatican being destroyed by a bomb made of antimatter.'

'Wrong again,' said Wangley, 'definitely not Rome ...'

'In which case,' suggested his romantic partner, suppressing a sigh, 'it must have been the time you narrowly escaped death in Florence, in order to prevent the release of a new plague, following clues taken from Dante's *Divine Comedy* ...'

'It wasn't *that* ...' said the reputable professor.

'You know, darling,' said Susannah, 'now we think about it, isn't it about time you stop taking yourself to European capitals filled with dangerous ancient secrets? Why not stay at home and read a good book?'

Wangley nodded weakly, mopping his face again, and was about to concede that there might be something in that idea. But just then a voice spoke from the tannoy above their heads.

'Ladies and gentlemen,' it said, 'this is your captain speaking. Please fasten your seatbelts as we are now beginning our descent into Prague, the golden city, a place of mystery and magic.'

2

'... city of mystery and magic,' Wangley said, just two hours later, as he and Susannah settled into their Airbnb. 'During the reign of Rudolf II in the sixteenth century, half the alchemists in the world came to Prague. The city was filled with magicians, astrologers, artificers, people crafting magic spells and creating elixirs ...'

'Is that so?' said Susannah, manhandling her suitcase onto the bed and unzipping it. She began to lay out her clothes.

Their host, a gentle, elderly man in a faded cardigan, had finished showing them around and was preparing to exit.

'You won't have any trouble from your only neighbour on this floor,' he said. 'Dr Bialystock is a famous scientist — indeed, yes, a fellow academic. But he keeps to himself, and is quite deaf ...'

So saying, he bade them a happy stay in the City of a Hundred Spires, and went humming down the stairs.

'... indeed, right on this street here, is the famous Faust House,' Wangley continued, as though he had not been interrupted. 'Four hundred years ago, this was a known haunt of alchemists! And most famously of all, it was here that the devil is supposed to have reclaimed the soul of some poor sorcerer, leaving a smoking, smouldering hole in the roof. Just like he reclaimed Faust – hence the Faust House gets its name!'

'You don't say,' Susannah replied, as she arranged her outfit for the evening and then stepped into the shower.

'Not the *real* Faust, of course,' Wangley went on, the moment she returned. 'Many people do not realise that Johann Georg Faust was in fact a real person, rather than simply the creation of Christopher Marlowe or Goethe,' he enthused. 'He never came to Prague, though. But famous Masters of Magic truly *did* live there, including the famous British mystic Sir Clyffe Rycharde – who was also spy master to Queen Elizabeth I. A genuine international man of mystery!'

Susannah nodded absent-mindedly as she lay down on her back for a rest.

'It's said the Faust House has cabbalistic signs painted all over the walls …' Wangley persevered, with undiminished intensity.

'Richard, would you be an angel,' Susannah said, lifting one of the slices of cucumber she had placed over her eyes, 'and go out for a short walk just to give me a moment to prepare for my talk this evening?'

'Of course,' said the esteemed professor, 'you must have a chance to get ready. Forgive me, my love. It is a big occasion, the biggest of your life …'

'Bye then,' she said softly, already falling into a welcome slumber. 'Be sure to close the door after you!'

3

He did not think. He just acted.

When not performing the demanded action, he rested. Sometimes he grew hungry, and he ate.

Time passed.

He waited for the next instruction to arrive. Then, when it came, he was activated. He got up and went out into the street.

People feared him, and moved out of his way. They gave terrified glances as he walked to his destination.

What happened when he got there was a mystery. A blank. He could remember nothing.

And afterwards, he came straight back. Sometimes he was shaking, sometimes he needed to clean himself up. There were little injuries on him that needed time to heal. Although, being such a large and strong creature, he did not injure easily. Meaning that whatever had happened, must have been very …

Well. He could not remember. And he chose not to try. He knew that he only existed to do as he was told.

Perform the actions instructed by his master. His tasks were essential. They had to be done.

And that was good enough for him. Mere existence was enough.

When there were no instructions, he did not exist.

He sat, and stared. He ate enough food to survive.

And he waited.

4

'My god ... this is staggering ...' whispered Richard Wangley. He could not believe his eyes. His temples throbbed, his hands shook and his throat was dry. He could not believe that this was happening.

On his way out of the apartment, the well-known expert had realised he had nothing to read. The book he had brought with him on the trip was still in his suitcase, which was back in the bedroom, and therefore lay within what he had inwardly termed the Sphere of Disapproval, which (having vacated the room) he preferred not to penetrate.

Thus he had grabbed the only thing to hand, which was the publicist's notes for this evening's talk, and placed them in his pocket.

Stepping out onto the streets of Prague, he had enjoyed an edifying stroll in the early evening sunshine.

Although he was well travelled in Europe, Richard had not visited Prague before, but had long desired to. It was indeed a storied city, having survived occupation, invasion, religious revolution and the ravages of twentieth-century Europe's twin nemeses: Nazism and Soviet control ...

As he turned a corner, Wangley contemplated one of the most profound mysteries of all deeply historical places, and one to which even he did not know the answer. No matter what continent, what climate or what creed a city claimed its own, whether the cement was still wet or the foundations went back thousands of years before Christ, there was one universal fact that connected every major conurbation in civilisation, and as he contemplated the conundrum a wry grin spread across the well-known professor's reasonably handsome face.

Before him stood Dennis O'Daly's pub.

How *was* it that Irish pubs proliferated with such remorseless success? He sometimes felt that if he stood at the Great Pyramid of Giza or the Temple of the Golden Pavilion in Kyoto, he would still be only a hundred yards from an inn called Michael McGrath's, or something similar.

Deciding that resistance to their ubiquity was futile (and also that the stocky men standing outside the Czech bar further up the street were intimidating) he pushed open the door and went in.

5

Moving inside, Wangley (who had visited the capital of the Emerald Isle) noted that it was not an entirely faithful recreation of a Dublin watering hole. Instead it seemed to be a sort of cross between a brightly lit sports bar and a karaoke joint.

Choosing the quietest corner to disappear into, he was soon nursing a glass of stout and reading the notes he had brought, which gave the details for tonight's event.

And what an event it seemed poised to be. The world's media had been alerted, and if any outlet failed to attend, they would regret it.

For Susannah was about to make an announcement that would cause a seismic shift in the world's understanding of science. Her chosen field, Nometic Science, had for decades been shunned by the mainstream scientific community and considered a fringe discipline.

That was about to change.

Until recently, the human brain's almost limitless untapped potential had been but a theory. However, working in a small independent laboratory with just a single lab assistant,

Susannah had found a way to detect and then harness the energy waves (she called them *nomes*) that were released by certain brain functions.

The implications were astounding. It meant that emotions had actual measurable weight. That thoughts really had the power to move objects and interact with matter. That sweet dreams really were made of something.

Once the discipline received adequate funding, it meant that human brains might be trained to perform everyday tasks such as switching on a light, reading a book or even playing the piano.

The possibilities were endless.

It was set to make front pages all over the world. Unusually, rather than release her results in a scientific paper, she had decided to incorporate her findings into a hardback book, which was deliberately written for a lay audience. And the publisher was determined to squeeze every possible ounce of publicity from the announcement.

Hence the international event, which was a combined press conference, book announcement and book launch all in one. Copies would be available around the world from the moment she finished speaking.

And when that moment came, conventional science would be turned on its head and would have a new celebrity. A new Stephen Hawking, but one who (with no disrespect to the famed scientist's physical challenges, Richard told himself) could shoot hoops with Obama, appear on *Hot Ones* and had the measurements 38–24–36.

Lengthy profiles of her were being written or planned by a host of major outlets, including *Time*, *Life*, *60 Minutes* and others that weren't synonyms for chronological duration.

Susannah Moses was about to become one of the most famous scientists of all time.

Wangley had known all this for weeks.

But now, reading through the notes for tonight's event (for which they'd booked out the Prague State Opera), his pulse started to race, his eyebrows shot up and he gripped the arm of his plastic chair so tightly he might have snapped it, were it not made of a high-tensile synthetic substance considerably more durable than human flesh.

'I've never seen anything like it,' he whispered. 'In all my thirty years working in this field!'

Quickly he was on the phone to Susannah's publicist.

'Is this true?' he asked. 'It can't be!'

'Well,' said Esmeralda Huntingdon-Cranthorpe, the publisher's elite PR, in her cut-glass British accent. 'What can I say. Just doing my job. They all RSVP'd.'

'*All* of them?' Wangley repeated.

As a Harvard professor, Wangley was the author of several books that were considered authoritative tomes within his own discipline. One or two were even stocked by the larger (city-centre flagship branch) chain bookstores that catered to the general reader. And, sure, they chugged along respectably in sales terms as the years went on, and they found themselves on required reading lists in various universities around the world.

But in academic circles, book launches (celebrating the fruit of half a dozen years' work, or even a whole decade's) were usually modest affairs in the quaint bookstores of Cambridge, Mass. Up to two dozen loyal friends in attendance quaffing warm white wine after a mercifully brief reading. If one's sales got into double figures for the night, one was tempted to break out the champagne.

'My god, the bishop of Prague is coming,' said Wangley. 'And Richard Dawkins? Aren't they natural enemies?'

'Susannah met them both in the Hamptons last summer,' said Esmeralda, 'and bonded over badminton.'

'Taylor *Swift*?' Wangley gasped.

'She follows Susannah on Insta,' she said. 'Reached out to ask for Susie's recipe for dry-rub barbecue gourd.'

'My gourd,' said Wangley. 'I mean, my god. I'm so …' he gulped. 'Proud of her.'

As he said this, he experienced a mysterious stabbing pain in his stomach, which he could not identify.

'Two Kardashians,' he whispered throatily.

'Just coincidence, really. They happen to be in town launching their new perfume and got wind of it. Didn't want to miss out.'

Wangley thanked her and rang off.

6

There was no doubt that Susannah's book was going to make waves. He had known this from the moment he read it.

It was going to move the dial and change the game. Push the envelope? It was going to place the envelope on a rocket into the stratosphere. And hopefully, that rocket would smash some glass ceilings on the way.

If not, it might bounce back and destroy us all. The thought made him shudder.

Richard was a tenured professor at Harvard and at the top of his profession. He had no problem with being in a relationship with a woman who was more successful than he was. He welcomed it.

He did. He welcomed it!

The relationship, still quite new, had come as a surprise. His friends had always regarded Richard as a 'confirmed bachelor'. Which doesn't always mean gay, Richard was keen to point out, even though (he was even more keen to point out) there's nothing wrong with being gay, which he wasn't. He'd always rather go to bed with a warm cup of cocoa and the latest issue of *Symboligistical American* than a muscled, strapping, linseed-oil-covered athlete — but that's not important. He just wasn't gay.

But then a little over a year ago a chance meeting with Susannah, whom he'd known for several decades, had unexpectedly blossomed into something beautiful.

And all of a sudden, well into his fifties, Richard was in love.

You never knew what to expect in life. It always threw you a curveball. And what mattered was whether you were going to hit that ball for a home run — or swing and miss, and return to the dugout red-faced with shame. Accompanied by the boos of the crowd. And possibly a tossed drinks cup filled with something unpleasant smelling.

It was wonderful having a partner after all these years.

Someone to talk to at the end of the day. Even if she did have the disconcerting habit of suddenly guffawing when he was speaking passionately.

Of course, one had to get used to a new partner's habits. That was the deal. Such as the way she *did* like to keep those earbuds of hers in, even at mealtimes. And in bed. *Her* bed, that is.

Richard had perhaps expected a little longer of a 'honeymoon period' before they started sleeping in separate beds, in separate rooms. But life — and love — were all about compromise. It was a learning process. And his whole life had been about learning.

When you stop learning, that's when it's just about time for them to throw you in the coffin and slam the lid, that's what he liked to say. In fact, it was when reciting this favourite mantra that he had first heard that incongruous guffaw.

That's what he loved about her. Always full of surprises.

She seemed to have so many hobbies as well, and was hardly ever home. Sometimes a week went past and he hardly set eyes on her. Well, that just showed how lucky he was, to be with such a popular woman!

Now Susannah was poised to launch what would be one of the most revolutionary scientific books since Darwin's *On the Origin of Species* ...

He could not be more thrilled. He wanted everyone to hear about it.

And that reminded him.

There was one person in Prague he had yet to tell. Someone he had been looking forward to catching up with – a professor who had been something of a mentor in years gone by.

Wangley had been supervised by him for a year when he had been doing a post-doctoral at Budapest University, and ever since then, Wangley had made sure to keep in touch with emails, birthday cards and Christmas round robin letters.

His mentor, Jaroslav Sedlak, was not quite the correspondent that Wangley had been. In fact, now he really thought about it, Richard could not recall receiving a single reply to any of the messages over the years. But then, the old professor was a busy bee, and undoubtedly had higher things in his mind. Just the thought of seeing him again filled Wangley's heart with warmth.

Sedlak had always been something of an eccentric, and he could be endearingly cranky at times.

'Vangly! Vy must you constantly dog my every vaking moment, you facking nuisanz?!' was a frequent complaint, Richard remembered, with an indulgent chuckle.

But his insight, intelligence and integrity made just one minute with Sedlak more gratifying than an hour with any other equally senior academic.

He had sent an email warning the old fellow that he was inbound, and not having received a response, now he decided to try and google him.

The results were naturally in Czech, and Richard (a confirmed Luddite when it came to all these newfangled pieces of machinery that seemed to dominate people's lives these days) struggled with autotranslate. It seemed there was a bevy of Jaroslav Sedlaks within Prague.

But (shaky as Richard's understanding of Czech was) unless he'd undergone gender transition and retrained as a judge, started playing Under-18s basketball for the Prague Beelzebubs or been given a suspended sentence for importing tainted watermelons, the man had gone to ground.

'Where is he?' Richard wondered.

A horrible doubt sprang up in him. He recalled Jaroslav telling of heart disease running in his family, and (then a man in late middle-age) frequently complaining of chest pains.

The years were not kind to any of us, Wangley thought. *They could be polite, inscrutable, even deceptively obsequious — but never kind. And Jaroslav must be well into his seventies by now.* Suddenly his mentor's silence seemed ominous. *I will keep looking for him*, he told himself, *but emotionally, I ought to prepare for the worst* ...

Richard took another sip from his glass of stout.

His recent exposure to the discipline of Nometic Science had given him a new perspective on the world. He had learned to try and spot uncanny and unexplained events that might be omens presaging important happenings. *Look out for things that never usually happen*, was Susannah's advice.

Once you knew how to spot them, you became sensitive to the fact that they were all around you.

Looking up from his drink, he saw a group of calm and sensible-looking young men at the next table, all in clean, well-pressed clothes.

'Let's finish our soft drinks and go back to the hotel,' one of the men was saying. 'We want to be fresh in the morning for yoga. And I want to enjoy this stag weekend to the absolute limit. We're here to honour the union of Darren and Kylie, not engage in riotous bacchanalia …' The others all nodded in agreement.

'And let's not forget, we are representing Wakefield on the international stage here,' said another.

'That's a responsibility we don't want to take lightly,' said a third. 'Imagine giving Czech people a bad impression of Englishmen.'

They all shook their heads.

Not knowing quite sure why, Richard felt a certain disquiet.

He turned to look the other way and found himself looking at a table at which three drinkers were sitting solemnly in front of untouched pints. They were a priest, a rabbi and an imam, in full regalia. He nodded at them (and assumed that at least one of those pints was the widely celebrated 0.0% Guinness).

They stared back at him with fixed expressions.

Although he was only a beginner in Nometic Science, and the corresponding fields of Extra Sensory Perception and presentiment, Richard started to feel there was a strange energy in this room.

He rose and went back into the street.

Little did he know that he was stepping into a maelstrom.

7

'What's going on? Someone tell me!' Richard yelled. His heart was hammering, his armpits sweating and his nostrils quivering.

From within a mass of uniformed officers, a plainclothes detective stepped forward. He was tall, gruff and unshaven, with a hangdog expression and a Gitanes cigarette on his lips.

'You are ...?' he asked.

'I'm an American citizen!' said Richard. 'My name is Richard Wangley, and I'm staying at this address. Please, you must tell me what is happening!'

The detective had tired eyes – eyes that were tired from seeing a thousand crime scenes. It was an unfortunate coincidence that today, on his first day off for nineteen weeks, his girlfriend had insisted he take her round Prague's Oppressive Crime Scene Photography Exhibition. Especially after such a long week. During which he had been sent on a refresher course in Oppressive Crime Scene Photography Analysis.

Looking into his despairing eyes, Wangley began to fear the worst.

Before the detective could speak, the crowd of officers parted as two people carried a covered stretcher down the stairs and out into the street. On it was the distinctive bulk of a human body, not moving, and covered head to toe.

Richard had turned the corner into the street where his and Susannah's Airbnb was located with a tune on his lips and a spring in his step. Then he had stopped dead, horrified by what was in front of him.

The street was filled with flashing lights, and a crowd of onlookers was being held back by police tape. As Richard approached, an ambulance was pulling up between two police vans.

He had rushed over, but in the melee, failed to get his voice heard. He almost had to fight his way to the front of the crowd, where he saw, to his horror, the front door to his own residence hanging off its hinges.

It looked like it had been shattered inwards with a battering ram.

'What happened?' Richard asked again, insistently.

By some strange alchemy of crowds, everyone at that moment, who had been arguing and talking so vociferously, all grew quiet. At the same moment the stretcher was lowered to the ground and a forensic pathologist stepped from the back of the ambulance.

The hushed crowd, reverent in the visible presence of death, watched as the forensic scientist took the corpse's pulse and made a note of the time.

My god, thought Richard. *Susannah? It can't be!*

Then the forensic scientist drew back the sheet.

'Oh my GOD!' he screamed. 'LOOK at this. This is so GROSS.'

The crowd shuddered. Richard thought he was going to faint.

'I mean, who would DO this?' asked the pathologist, to the heavens. A fellow medic whispered something in his ear, and he snapped back: 'No, I mean who would do THIS JOB? Why am I having to look at the horrible dead bodies all the time! Especially when they've been ... Urgh ... My mother was right. "Otakar," she said, "be a baker like your father!" Early mornings, yes, but early mornings I could handle compared to seeing people's – ugh! – dragged out of their ...' He put his hand over his mouth to repress a gag reflex.

'I am Detective Rulka of the Czech Constabulary,' said the hangdog police officer. 'You were staying at this residence?'

'That is correct,' said Richard, dry-mouthed. 'I can prove it. My possessions are inside.'

'So this is your passport?' asked the police officer, holding it out. Richard nodded, then patted his pocket, surprised he'd gone out without it. 'And this is your copy of a book called ...' Rulka examined the jacket: *'The Manosphere: Why Feminazis and Woketards Are Cucking Your Balls Off.'*

The detective's voice rang out over the crowd. Richard moved awkwardly from foot to foot.

'Ah, yeah,' he said. 'I mean, I think so.'

'Quotes on the back. "This guy tells it like it really is" – Jordan Peterson. "I give this important book a rating of Five Penises out of Five" – Andrew Tate.'

'Yeah, I, uh, that is definitely mine,' said Richard. 'I mean I wouldn't necessarily describe myself as a Manosphere kind of *guy*, you know what I mean? I just wanted to be sort of, informed in the debate, really. My brother-in-law talks about this stuff, you see, and ...' Richard leaned closer to the detective and said in a low, reasonable voice: 'I just wanted to be able to say, "Hank, I don't agree with you, and this is why." You know?'

The cop was looking at him curiously. Richard tried to swallow. 'My girlfriend was here. She's also American. Is she okay?'

'What does she look like?' asked the cop.

'Light brown hair,' Wangley said. 'Curly. All natural. She's forty but I guess you'd say she looked about thirty-six. Maybe thirty-four or thirty-three depending on the light …'

'This is the body of an elderly man,' said the cop. 'We found no female at the property.'

'Oh my god,' Richard gasped. His whole body sagged. He was aware that he was babbling with nerves, which was a regrettable tendency of his when face to face with authority. As a white middle-class, middle-aged man, he fundamentally approved of the police and thought they did a good job. Finding himself at a crime scene being stared at by an officer, he suddenly felt like he was skidding on ice.

'But wait,' he said, 'she's not here? Where did she go?'

'I do not know, Mr Vangly.'

'Actually, it's "Professor". I'm a professor at Harvard University.'

The policeman's hangdog expression seemed somehow to hang even deeper.

'The body appears to be that of a Dr Bialystock, your next-door neighbour. The violence inflicted was …' He turned and looked to the pathologist, who as he examined the injuries had not left off lamenting.

'Severe lacerations to the lateral … My GOD … how do you even DO THAT to a … Contusions in the … Oh my …

when will it end ... Blunt-force trauma to the – well, here comes my dinner ...'

There was an unpleasant sound of something wet arriving on concrete and the crowd (who, staring at a murder scene as they were, one might have thought were hardened to such things) produced a dismayed groan.

Richard rapidly gave his and his girlfriend's details to Detective Rulka. Then he stood a while feeling dazed, wondering who he should call. He ought to speak to the American embassy at once, probably. But it was out of office hours, and by the time they opened in the morning who knew what developments there might have been in the case?

For all he knew, she could have popped out for a soda when the murder had happened, and might arrive round the corner at any second, just as surprised as anyone else. The sudden knowledge that he was kidding himself and this wasn't going to happen made a sob rise in Richard's throat.

Okay, just stay calm, he told himself. *I need fresh air, and a chance to think. I must get away from this ghoulish crowd ...*

'And what he's done to the EYES!' wailed the pathologist, as Richard retreated.

8

Walking along the night-time streets, without knowing where to go, Richard wondered what to think. Susannah had been snatched by someone or some group, for reasons he couldn't imagine.

On this night of all nights.

But maybe, he started to think, the event tonight was the reason. It was somehow connected with her book, and her scientific breakthrough ...

Was she still alive? Was she suffering somewhere, afraid and alone? Or asleep and unconscious?

She had certainly made revelations in her book that theoretically threatened the world order and established power structures, as well as all religions. Potent enemies indeed, any one of whom might have decided she needed to be silenced.

This dark thought filled his heart with foreboding.

But then, Wangley thought, *her book has already been printed.*

It had been translated into multiple languages and was poised to be published in dozens of territories in a few hours' time. Nothing, even a continent-spanning multi-agency conspiracy involving the CIA and the secret police forces of multiple countries, could realistically prevent the book's propagation.

If anything, her disappearance would *spread* the book's fame like wildfire.

And that wildfire – would backfire.

Could it be a false flag attack, then? A deliberate ploy for publicity, just like the one that fans considered Agatha Christie had pulled off in 1928, when she had vanished for a week just before the publication of her masterpiece, *The Murder of Roger Ackroyd*? It had made Christie front-page worldwide news, and had sent her fame into the stratosphere.

Would Susannah be so cold as to attempt the same?

Impossible. Especially not if she had to commit a murder into the bargain …

Wangley decided he ought to call Tasmine Buckthorne-Minghella, or whatever the posh British publicist was called.

He dialled her number but it was busy. The evening launch event was only two hours away. She must be in the middle of final preparations – Kardashians and Taylor Swift inbound.

Then he had a thought. A thought that made him gasp. And shiver. If Susannah really had unlocked the potential of the human mind, then there was every chance that right now she would be trying to use that skill to send him a message through the ether. Trying with every ounce of her might. All he had to do was make himself a receptive antenna.

'Come on!' Richard called loudly, returning her mental energy with psychic efforts of his own. He stared up at the clouds, gripping his cell phone. 'Come on, Susannah! Message me!'

A family happened to be drifting past at that moment, looking for a restaurant for their evening meal.

'Oh no,' he said, seeing them, and realising how it must look. 'I'm not some desperate loser waiting for a woman to text me back. You see, I'm trying to make my actual girlfriend send me messages *using her mind*.' He tapped the side of his head and grinned at them. 'You see?'

They kept walking without meeting his eye.

Then his phone buzzed. He gasped. He was so startled, he nearly dropped it.

There was a text from an unknown number.

'My old friend,' the message said, 'so good to hear from you. Meet me at the Nasraksa Bar near the Astronomical Clock, in an hour? Sedlak.'

9

Wangley's heart filled with relief. A friendly voice, at such an hour. Just when he needed it.

First, of course – he must keep trying to alert the organisers of tonight's event.

The publicist, Tabitha Whattington-Christmasstree, had said on multiple occasions in Richard's hearing that she thrived on stress and claimed never to be happier than when solving a problem. If that was genuinely the case, then tonight would turn out to be a real treat for her.

Richard imagined the rows of celebrities waiting in increasingly tense silence for the author's appearance. He saw the towering piles of unsigned books beside dozens of bottles of prosecco in silver buckets filled with rapidly melting ice.

Her number was still busy. After trying her five more times, Richard gave up. He saw he was getting near to his rendezvous with Sedlak and made a mental note to phone the publicist again as soon as possible.

He was at the venue in a few minutes. The burly men at the door hardly acknowledged his entry, and he sat in a booth beneath one of the broad stone arches that formed the underground bar.

He looked at everyone who passed, but recognised nobody.

'Dr ... Wangford?' said a voice. A decidedly feminine one.

Richard looked up. Before him was an elegant-looking woman in her early thirties with long, mahogany-coloured hair. She was dressed simply in a low-cut white T-shirt, old blue jeans and leather jacket, but there was something about her that looked professional, intelligent – and laser focused.

'I ...' Richard was wrongfooted. The text message had been signed just 'Sedlak'. But, he now wondered, could it have been sent by a different Sedlak, from a different generation? Someone who had access to her father's (or grandfather's) mobile phone, perhaps? Richard could not for the life of him remember whether his old mentor had children or not ...

His heart leapt again, as he contemplated what this might mean for his friend. Incapacity, injury, the cold hand of death?

'I am ... Richard Wangley,' he said cautiously, choosing for some reason not to rebuke this attractive young woman for her inaccuracy about his title, as he had the policeman minutes earlier.

'I thought it was you!' she said. 'I see you are alone ... may I join you?'

The down-lighting in the underground bar sharply accentuated the curves of the individual in front of him, even more so when she threw her jacket over one shoulder and put her hand on one hip. And then span in a pirouette that turned into a belly dance. She finished by winking at the barman who threw an olive twenty feet across the bar where she caught it in her cleavage and then (by a minutely controlled muscular contraction) made it leap quivering into the air so she could catch it in her teeth before devouring it.

Richard gulped.

He wondered what his girlfriend would say if she could see him consorting and indeed cavorting with such an exotic female specimen, just minutes after she had apparently vanished from the surface of the earth.

If he had any shred of decency, he would surely ask her to leave at once, and not come back.

'Please, sit down,' he said. 'I insist.'

10

'My name is Marika Novak,' she said, oozing onto the banquette.

'New,' said Richard.

'Not at all,' she replied, throwing the threadbare leather jacket down on the seat beside her. 'It's practically falling to pieces.'

'No, your name. It means "new",' he said, with a roguish smile.

'It really is true what they say about you,' Marika returned. 'As interesting and insightful in person as you are in your books.'

Once Marika had arrived, the barman (who until now had regarded Richard as so much human wallpaper) had suddenly become interested in his job. Within milliseconds of the seat of her buttocks pressing into the cushion, the pair were both furnished with drinks and complimentary snacks. The lights were turned to a moody, flattering dimness and the music turned on.

Richard had been in the process of eating an olive when Marika said this, and her words (or to be precise, the effect of the meaning of them) caused it to get caught in his throat.

'You've read one of my books?'

'You've heard of one of my books?'

'You've heard of an author with my name?'

All three questions simultaneously bottlenecked in the throat of a man already struggling with a potentially life-threatening (but at the very least exceptionally ticklish) obstruction.

Wangley coughed modestly, and then (realising the trouble, or the olive stone, was situated deeper than he'd realised) did so again very violently, removing the obstruction. This made his eyes bulge and rasped his throat. The lights glared his eyes momentarily.

He swallowed and blinked.

'You've heard of me?' he asked, at the same time as a ting! announced the arrival of the olive stone he'd just coughed out in a wine glass forty feet down the room. A table of diners near where the olive landed offered a polite round of applause.

'But of *course*!' said Marika quite crossly. 'You are famous in America, no?'

'No,' said Wangley ruefully.

'But you are millionaire author of books about art, yes?'

'No,' said Wangley again. 'Just "author" covers it.'

'In Europe, we value our academics,' Marika responded. 'They are titans of society. Here in Czechia, we make a playwright our first democratic leader.'

'And in America we elect cowboy actors and reality stars,' said Wangley, deciding to go no further in this strain of conversation because a thriller parody is no place for political discourse.

There were televisions all along the bar, and, without Richard realising it (because he never looked at them), in the last few minutes they had started showing footage from a local crime scene.

It was the scene from which he had recently fled. Across the screen ran a message reading: NEW EVIDENCE – MAIN SUSPECT – RICHARD WANGLEY.

Photos of him suddenly filled the screen, along with specific details: born 1967, height 5 foot 9, hair colour light brown, favourite ice cream vanilla, Superman underpants, one nostril larger than other ...

'No one recognises me!' he said. 'It literally never happens.'

Richard's fingerprints now filled the screen. Detailed descriptions of his movements and habits followed. 'Wanted for MURDER' ran like police tape across top and bottom. At the bar, one bored-looking man poured a vodka for a customer, while the customer stared into space, possibly following the progress of a fly against the ceiling lights.

'I do,' she said. 'And in fact – I need your help.'

'I just can't imagine anyone ever recognising me – an academic and author of works of art history,' said Richard modestly, as the screen was filled with images of his books above the legend, 'MURDER SUSPECT AUTHOR OF WORKS OF ART HISTORY', and 'Amazon reviews proclaim books arrived on time and in good condition despite author's suspected culpability' ...

'You mean your appearance here is just a coincidence? You weren't sent?' he asked urgently.

'What do you mean?' she asked.

He told her that he had been invited here to see an old friend.

'I don't know about that,' she said, not interested in his personal dilemmas. 'All I know is I was told to come to a place near here to receive a message. I'm very nervous. I came into this bar because I was a minute early, and to gather my thoughts. Then I saw you.'

'Go on,' he said, 'tell me what's wrong.'

'Thank you,' she said. 'You see, I'm afraid someone means me harm ...'

11

Richard's instinctive hatred of injustice reared its head.

'Just tell me what I can do to help,' he said.

Behind the bar, one of the stultified barmen had turned the volume up on the TV.

'We are hearing that the serious murder suspect Richard Wangley, pictured, is wanted by the police for the extremely violent slaying of a sweet, innocent resident of southern Prague, a man who did nothing to harm anyone and also loved kittens.'

The barman stared at one of the screens, open mouthed.

'Loved kittens, not in a weird sexual way,' the voiceover said. 'Like, in a lovely, gentle, sweet, old-man way. And now he's gone. Taken from us by this monster.'

'Presumed monster,' said another anchor, piping up.

'Yes, that's right. It's just presumption that this clearly evil man is a monster. Whose picture we are showing now. We repeat, this is Richard Wangley, professor of symbological secrologist studies …'

'Walk with me through the town square?' Marika said. 'I have to go that way and I'm afraid that's where I'm in danger.'

'Of course,' said Richard.

The barman turned the volume up again and popped an almond in his mouth.

'This just in,' said the second host. 'It seems we are hearing from several sources that this presumed murderer is drawn to underground bars. And drinks lager beer. He tends to sit in a north-facing seat in the third booth from the door and wear a cream rollneck sweater under a maroon single-breasted pleated linen jacket with a distinctive Lisbon lapel. He also habitually wears a defensive smirking expression...'

'That's right, Janusz,' frothed his on-air partner. 'The details about this modern-day Hannibal Lecter keep coming...'

'Despite the fact that Hannibal Lecter himself is from the modern day, Lina. Perhaps you are thinking of the Hannibal of antiquity who rode elephants over the Alps into Rome...' chuckled the first TV presenter.

'I am not,' said the second presenter, beaming. 'But thank you for explaining my thoughts to me.'

'Just a joke, Lina!' said the other, smiling into the camera.

'Like the joke where you said you would leave your wife?' asked Lina, laughing uproariously and punching the other presenter in the arm.

A paper was handed to the pair on-screen. Janusz scanned it and read fresh revelations to camera.

'... we are now hearing he likes sitting gawping at television sets in bars where his description is being read out, and in fact that he is STANDING UP NOW!'

Richard had an itch and needed to stand.

The barman, staring at the screen, crunched another almond.

At that moment emergency services vehicles came screeching along the street and parked outside. Their flashing lights glared through the ankle-level windows that allowed light into the restaurant basement, causing a beam of blue to flash in the underground space.

One of the street-facing windows the lights flashed through happened to advertise the availability of Red Rum. And a large mirror being behind the underground bar, reflecting the slanting light, meant that as Richard rose from his seat, 'MUR DER' flashed in red on his chest.

'He's getting up now!' said the television. 'Look! It's him right there! Jesus Wenceslas Christ …'

'Pick up my tab, please?' Richard asked.

The barman held out a card machine without turning round.

'If you turn around now and see you will CATCH a MURDERER!' cried the voice on the screen.

Wangley placed a couple of notes in the tip jar and, adjusting his jacket so it sat nicely on his shoulders, and checking his reflection, followed Marika out onto the street, stopping halfway up the stairs to street level, to sniff a potted clematis.

'He's gone!' said the TV host. 'You just can't tell some people.'

'You can't indeed, Janusz,' sighed his colleague. 'Happy wedding anniversary, by the way. Sport now …'

Overhead, the fly continued to buzz against the light.

The barman popped another almond into his mouth.

12

'Where now?' asked Wangley. He was happy to have a moment's distraction from the maelstrom of his emotions.

Although he'd been waiting for his old mentor, as he sat in the bar he had started to get a strange feeling he was being watched, or that something or someone was paying close attention to him. He couldn't quite put his finger on why.

If Sedlak did indeed turn up to the Nasraksa Bar expecting to find him there, Wangley hoped his old friend would forgive him his absence. But Richard was a man of the old school, and firmly believed that a woman in distress trumped all other concerns. The idea of a knight in shining armour was a tad old fashioned these days, but sometimes when one heard the call it was impossible to resist.

'If that makes me a sexist, then gosh dang it, I guess I am one,' he told himself.

(He was.)

He followed Marika a few yards along a winding street and turned a corner. The crowds were growing thicker now. They came out into a public square and Wangley caught his breath.

'My god!' he said. 'It's magnificent!'

Before him was one of the mechanical marvels of the European Middle Ages, and undoubtedly one of the grandest sights in all Prague: the Astronomical Clock. Finished in 1410, the clock was said to have been running without stopping since 1496.

It had a minute hand, an hour hand, and further measures for the day, and even the passage of the months was recorded by a dial showing the different signs of the zodiac.

The timepiece was also decorated by numerous mystical and occult illustrations and figures, whose precise meaning was obscure. As it called the hour, four clockwork puppets (representing different human sins) came to life to shake their heads forebodingly at the assembled public.

There was a Turk, a miser with a pot of gold, a man looking in a mirror, and Death (who rang the hour). At the same moment, figures of the apostles (two mysteriously missing) marched past an empty window above the clock.

It made for a magical sight, and crowds always gathered on the hour to watch this spectacle that was half enchanting and half eerie.

'It is said,' Wangley told Marika, 'that the town council of Prague were so delighted by the clock that they wanted to ensure no other city had one like it, and that they had the clockmaker blinded to ensure he never made another ...'

'I know this,' she said, looking at him oddly. 'I am from Prague. You do not have to tell me such things ...'

As she spoke, the reasons for the press of the crowd became apparent as the clock began to strike the hour. The two or three hundred people watching fell silent. But the striking of the clock was not perfectly audible, as there were another thousand or so people milling through the Old Town square and sitting at the outdoor tables of the innumerable restaurants, drinking, talking and laughing.

'What am I doing here?' Wangley suddenly asked himself. 'My girlfriend has gone missing! I ought to be out looking for her, not sightseeing!'

Guilt, fear, anxiety flooded him. He felt a throbbing in his ears and started to get dizzy.

Then another thought struck him. *What if the police start suspecting* me *for her disappearance?*

But no, that seemed too farfetched. What exactly would a man do with someone he'd kidnapped just minutes after arriving in a foreign city for the first time?

Besides, he could account for his time while she had been snatched. Someone ought to remember him from his time in Dennis O'Daly's — although he *had* deliberately sat on his own and attracted as little notice as possible ...

The throbbing in his ears grew louder as the crowd pressed in closer and the clanging of the clock progressed ... The dizziness became more intense ...

And then there was a flash of something in the air and a shadow seemed to pass in front of the clock. There was a thump and a commotion. Then a scream of pure terror.

13

First it was one voice, then another, and within moments a whole chorus of wails sprang up.

The crowd seemed to press closer out of curiosity, but then a panic spread through the throng of tourists like the shiver of an electric shock. Professor Wangley felt the breath crushed out of him, and then people were surging away from the clock, trying to escape.

He was nearly knocked over and struggled to get his balance. He called out for Marika. As people rushed past he saw her on the ground nearby and helped her up.

'What is it?' she asked, shaken.

'Something fell ...' he said.

'The clock?' she asked. 'It is damaged?'

'No,' said Wangley. Looking up, he saw his words receiving a macabre echo in the Death Skeleton in the clockwork mechanism above, still shaking its head as the clock struck the hour ... 'I think it's something more alarming than that.'

Although afraid of what he might see, the esteemed professor couldn't help but be drawn closer to where the object had landed. Marika, holding his hand, came with him.

The crowd had almost entirely dispersed, except for a few aghast people covering their eyes with their hands, and one ghoul who had his phone out and was recording.

Wangley saw it was exactly as he had feared. There in front of him on the stone cobbles was the shattered body of a man, limbs broken, neck twisted. Horrifying as the spectacle was, he could not look away.

He came close to see if there was anything he could do, any first aid to administer. But it seemed horribly clear that this person was beyond help.

'No ...' whispered Marika. 'It is not possible ... It cannot be ... Why would they do this ...?'

'Don't look,' said Richard gently. 'I'm afraid he's dead ... He must have fallen ...' He looked upwards. But there did not seem anywhere to have fallen from, no window in the ancient stone tower (that of Prague's medieval town hall) wide enough for him to have fallen from.

And the body had landed a full fifteen feet out from the tower's wall. Too far, surely, for anyone but an Olympic athlete to jump.

He fell from the sky?

'Marika – don't look!' he said again, seeing that the woman was transfixed and unable to take her eyes away from the body.

'But I know him,' she said. 'This man – he is – he is famous ... *This is not possible!*'

Richard looked too. The poor fellow appeared to be twenty-five or so years old, fresh faced, dressed in anonymous enough clothes, a sweater and jeans. And, hardly understanding what he was seeing in the cognitive dissonance of the moment, Richard saw that something stuck out of the body's mouth.

A strand of something, cloth perhaps. The incongruity of this overwhelmed Richard's common sense and he pulled on it, almost persuading himself that if this obstruction was removed, the man might be able to breathe. Or speak.

In his hand was a clump of parchment. Hardly at all wet with saliva. It unfurled as he held it, assuming its natural shape.

'*PRAHA*,' it said across the top of the map, in a flowing hand.

'My god,' said Richard.

And he saw it was a map of medieval Prague.

14

Across the bottom of the map were written a number of symbols grouped together in what might be words.

'What does it say?' asked Marika. She was shivering, unable to think straight, and clearly going into shock.

The crowd had returned and formed a perimeter of sorts, near enough to watch, far enough to give a modicum of respectful distance to the dead body. There were shouts of officials trying to give orders, and the distant but approaching wail of sirens.

No longer silent, the crowd was a loud hubbub of chatter and speculation.

'It's not in any European language,' said Richard. 'In fact, it's cuneiform.'

'What was it doing in his mouth?' Marika asked.

'That's the question,' replied the renowned academic, looking down at the body. 'And where did *he* come from ...'

'Professor Wangley!' said a voice through a loudhailer. 'Step away from the body.'

'What?' Richard said, spinning round. He was disconcerted to find he recognised the voice. 'How do they know my name?'

'Stand back!' came the voice, which he now recognised was that of Rulka, the cop from the crime scene. He was speaking in English, which even in the few hours he had been in the city, Wangley had already noticed was the lingua franca, especially in tourist areas.

'Professor Wangley is wanted for murder and kidnapping! He is a violent and dangerous armed suspect!' yelled Detective Rulka. Intending by these words, perhaps, to get the crowd to withdraw in a respectful and dignified manner.

People started panicking, screaming and rushing in every direction.

'Be calm while I take this murderer into custody!' bellowed the policeman. 'I shall now fire my gun to ensure orderly behaviour!'

There was a gunshot.

Pandemonium broke out.

15

Why do they want me for the murder? Wangley thought. Albeit the thought was not as elegant and formally syntactical as this. It was more like: 'Wwwwwhhhhhfooooouuuuurrrr-gggghhhhffffuuuuck!'

Before he could think, he was running through the crowd. Self-preservation kicked in, and when he realised what he was doing he ducked behind an open-air restaurant table where a waiter was leaning over to light a candle for two patrons.

'Stop!' yelled Rulka, firing at Wangley.

The candle flickered to life and the waiter looked confusedly at the lighter in his hand, which he had not yet clicked. In the tourist shop yards behind, a shelf of clay figures exploded.

'Keep going – to that alleyway!' said Marika's voice, and to his amazement Wangley realised he still had not let go of her hand.

They sprinted and reached the alleyway, as another bullet hammered into the ancient Czech limestone of the wall opposite. Limestone that had been carved out of its quarry with rough tools, carefully dressed, transported and then laid with immense care and skill under the watchful eye of a master architect. Or his assistant (if he was ill that day), forming part of the overall magnificence that made Prague such a miraculous work of artistic grandeur, and a destination for tourists from around the world.

Now the bullet gouged out a shard of that limestone, and spat it at the two fugitives, accompanied by a shower of dust.

They got to an arch halfway down the passage and leant against a metal door, panting.

'I don't want to get you in trouble,' said Wangley. His head was still spinning. This was all so fast. One moment he was wondering if the police might possibly suspect him. Seconds later, he was evading arrest.

'I'm already in trouble,' Marika said. 'Lots of it.'

The metal door opened behind them and they both tumbled backwards, to the surprise of a teenage youth from the restaurant, who was taking out two large bags of rubbish.

Inside, to their left was the front of the restaurant where the bemused waiter still stood, shaking his lighter and frowning. To their right, was a large bustling kitchen where flames were shooting up beneath frying pans, and gouts of steam roiled above enormous pots. A dozen unfriendly male faces stared back, with light glinting off carving knives and cleavers.

In front of them a stone staircase led downwards.

'Down here,' said Wangley, rushing forwards. 'Wow, they've got some nice wines. Which way now?'

As with many restaurants in Prague's Old Town, its ground-floor dining area was modest in comparison with its cavernous underground space. Luxuriously large dining rooms extended on both left and right, with perhaps fifty diners in each.

Between the two, and at the bottom of the stairs, was a waiting station with a till, a wine rack and some climbing plants on a trellis. Behind this, almost unnoticeable in the background, was a heavy-looking metal door.

'Stop!' yelled a voice from the top of the stairs and another shot rang out. Instantly everyone in the restaurant ducked, screamed and knocked their wine glasses over. A jet of sparks went up from the handle of the iron door, which swung open backwards. In moments Marika and Wangley were through it and descending into deep darkness.

'Where does this go?' asked Wangley, trying to watch his footing. A twisted ankle now, and he was done for.

'The whole of Prague is threaded through with these old tunnels,' Marika's voice came to him through the darkness. 'They are not usually used. They pretty much go everywhere …'

16

They held hands as they jogged forwards, so that they wouldn't lose each other in the darkness and give themselves away by calling out to each other.

The bottom of the staircase had given onto a tunnel that ran in both directions, with a curved stone ceiling above. Beneath his feet, Wangley was surprised to find cobblestones – then he remembered that seven hundred years before, this had been the street level. Before a disastrous flood had caused the whole city to be rebuilt a storey higher.

'You might be surprised to find yourself on cobblestones,' Marika said. 'But in fact this used to be street-level ...'

'That's okay,' Richard said. 'I just remembered that fact, so we're all caught up.'

Wangley and Marika followed the tunnel until it turned and the last glimmer of light from behind them had vanished.

They kept on, unsure where they were going.

'You said you knew that man,' said Wangley. 'You mean, personally?'

'No, no,' said Marika. And her voice was shaky again. 'I

mean – he is famous in the Czech Republic. His face is universally known …'

'What does he do? He's young. Is he an actor?' Wangley couldn't think how else someone so young could be famous across the country. There was no royal family, after all. 'Or a sports star?' he suggested. 'Perhaps a social media guy?'

'No,' Marika said. 'You don't understand what makes this impossible. He was famous long before social media. He was the great hope of the Czech economy – a tech genius and a national hero. He created some of the biggest businesses in the country. A whole industry sprung up at his fingertips. Everybody looked up to him. And then the dot-com bubble burst and everything went to hell. He disappeared.'

Wangley stopped. Marika was yanked to a halt by his hand. 'That doesn't make sense,' he said. 'The dot-com bubble was a generation ago. That man looked to be in his early twenties.'

'You're finally getting it,' breathed Marika in the quiet darkness of the tunnel. 'That man is Lukas Prochezka,' Marika said. 'His disappearance was a national mystery that everyone has been trying to solve for over twenty years.'

17

'Twenty years!' exclaimed Wangley. 'But that's impossible!'

'He disappeared off the face of the Earth in 2001,' Marika said.

Richard's head span.

'It's impossible!' he said.

'It appears to strain credulity,' conceded Marika.

'Just crazy!' Richard insisted. 'And then all of a sudden he just fell out of the sky tonight?'

'Like I said: not something I would have formerly regarded as possible,' said Marika.

Wangley gasped. 'But he looked like he hadn't aged a day!'

It just didn't seem possible.

'It doesn't strike me as . . .' Professor Wangley searched for the word. He could hardly catch his breath in his astonishment.

'Credible? Plausible?' asked Marika.

Richard shook his head.

'Possible?' she added.

Richard gasped.

She had expressed his feelings perfectly.

18

'I've been surprised by some twists in my time,' said Richard, trying to get his head round this enormous revelation, 'but—'
At this point, he was struck by the biggest twist of all.

19

It was a twist that Richard had not seen coming.

For the tunnel had turned left in the darkness, and Richard, walking in a straight line, had not. Thus he was hit very hard on the crown of his head by the rock that blocked his path.

Suddenly the total blanketing darkness of an underground tunnel in a foreign city didn't seem quite so friendly. Clutching his grazed scalp, he felt his way along the tunnel's wall. He suddenly felt a chill, as though this place were unwelcoming. Uncanny, even supernatural.

'Come on,' he said, 'let's keep going. I'm getting the shivers.'

'Me too,' said Marika. 'I feel something very disturbing is going on.' Her teeth chattered as she spoke.

Wangley removed his jacket and insisted she wear it, as hers had been dropped somewhere far behind. He also briefly outlined his experiences earlier in the evening. Marika shared his bewilderment.

'Now I understand why the police knew your name,' she said. 'Someone has done this deliberately to frame you. Do you have any enemies?'

'No, none,' Wangley said.

They walked on a few paces, then something occurred to him.

'Except maybe the Illuminati,' he said. 'Had a little run-in with them.'

'Oh!'

'The Rosicrucians too, now I think of it,' said Wangley. 'And Opus Dei.'

'Right,' said Marika, wondering who she had got herself mixed up with.

'Them, the Freemasons, the Knights Templar and the Vatican. And at various times a few different world governments and law enforcement agencies.'

Marika opened her mouth to respond, then hesitated to see whether the list was complete.

'Also the World Health Organization,' Richard went on, 'the World *Wealth* Organization, and Heinz.'

'Heinz?'

'Absolutely. Vexatious litigation, my left foot! My racketball game was completely *ruined* for six months. Of *course* they're liable for me slipping on soup I'd accidentally spilled myse—'

'I see,' she said. 'You injured yourself?'

'My left foot,' Wangley explained, pointing to it. (Marika could not see this.)

'And those are the only enemies you have?'

'That I know about,' he replied.

He felt they were deep enough into the tunnels now, and far enough from law enforcement, for him to turn the light in his phone on. It produced a small cone of light that made the large darkness ahead even more enormous.

'What sort of uses are these tunnels put to?' he asked.

'Anything you can think of, and a few more,' she replied.

'I think I hear something,' he said. 'The tunnels ahead might be in use. Tread quietly, and go behind me.'

There was some light coming from beneath a door in a side-passage. Hoping that it might be a way back onto the street and allow them to blend into society again, they approached with caution.

Wangley reached out and touched the metal surface of a door, which swung gently inwards. He saw he was looking into some sort of underground laboratory. There was a woman in a white overall in the background, checking readouts on a large machine against a clipboard in her hand.

In the foreground, however, much more arrestingly, there was a handsome man in a formal jacket and tie, lying on a table. His wrists and ankles were fastened there by metal bands, and his head was leaning upwards, as with consternation he watched the progress of a thick yellow laser. It appeared to be melting clean through the metal table, and it was gradually progressing between his outstretched legs, towards his torso.

'You want me to talk, Silverfinger?' he asked.

A portly red-haired man emerged from the shadows on the other side of the room.

'No, Mr Bond, I want you to apologise for the way you treated our receptionist!' He seemed to be thoroughly enjoying the other man's discomfort. 'She's an impressionable young woman, and also my wife's niece. There is such a thing as informed consent, Mr Bond. We are not in the 1960s, *Gott im Himmel*!'

The Secretest of Secretisms

As the laser sizzled ever closer to his trunk, the prisoner's panic reached boiling point.

'Why do I always get myself in these situations?' he said, apparently without realising he was speaking aloud. Something in his spirit seemed to alter and a new light glinted in his eyes.

'I should treat women respectfully, I realise that now!' he said. 'Stop the laser!'

The red-haired man appeared surprised and gave orders to his assistant at the machines. But there appeared to be some malfunction.

Amid the flurry of panic within the laboratory, Wangley whispered, 'Best leave these folks to their privacy.' He pulled the door to.

Marika followed as they quietly retraced their steps. A few seconds later there was an ear-splitting scream.

Then an exceedingly high-pitched voice rang out.

'I'll get you for this, Silverfinger!' it screamed. 'You virtue-signalling bastard!'

'Let's keep looking for another way out?' whispered Wangley.

Marika concurred.

20

Each night, after performing its dark deeds, the enormous being returned home and lay in darkness.

Waiting.

Waiting for the sound of screams to fade. Waiting for sleep to come. And waiting for the next instruction.

Except that, tonight, the darkness was pierced by the light from a lamp.

Alphonso Emmettio knew that that was his name. He had no need for more knowledge. He was an obedient servant. A tool of his master. The deeds he had to perform were essential. His master's will must be done.

But today, as he had stalked to the scene of his next deed, he had seen people noticing him. He had to make a difficult detour, which complicated and endangered the whole accomplishment.

And so for the first time he had started looking at the people on the street. To see how he could walk among them without being noticed.

He climbed onto a tram (which groaned and tilted in response to his weight) and saw the way people were. Some wore dark glasses, some wore hats and scarves. Some read books or listened to little devices in their ears. Some smiled or nodded their heads.

It would soon become impossible to perform his deeds if he kept on as he had been. He simply did not act like these people. He had to blend in more, or all would be lost.

He noticed clothes worn by men. He bought some of those, and discarded the dirty rags he had been wearing.

Bit by bit, he became more like them.

When it rained, they used umbrellas. He bought and broke three. The fourth he managed to work.

He had brought home a bunch of large tissues with writing on them. He saw some older people reading the tissues on public transport. They looked anonymous when they did that. He had to look anonymous. So with his empty hours he studied the letters and learned ...

In between, he received his instructions. Calls to perform his deeds. After the performance of which he felt a vague, weary sadness, and needed time to recover.

Each instruction was just a name, and an address.

He did not know how many more there would be.

He would keep going until he was told to stop. However many names there were.

He was an obedient being.

21

As Marika and Richard made their way through the darkness, Marika attempted to illuminate their thoughts with her explanations about the mysterious reappearing corpse.

'His name was Lukas Prochezka?' Wangley asked.

'Yes,' said Marika.

'And he was a, as you call it, *wunderkind*?' Wangley asked. 'A technological genius who built a whole industry in these very tunnels we are walking through? These abandoned old tunnels were the only spaces startup companies could afford to rent in the 1990s, and therefore the area became known as Prague's Silicon Basement? But those businesses all vanished almost as suddenly as they appeared, leaving these tunnels as they had been for the preceding six hundred years?'

'Yes, Richard,' said Marika, fatigued. 'Why must you repeat everything I said to you at length?'

'So that the same character is not talking constantly during a plot explanation sequence,' replied the senior academic, with a supercilious expression.

'Fascinating that a modern genius, creating new technologies, would make his home here,' said Richard. 'Hundreds of years earlier, these tunnels were also where the Prague alchemists were forced to work, to escape prosecution. They were the bleeding-edge scientists of their time, creating new inventions, crafting undreamt-of elixirs, away from the eyes of the law, making fortunes for themselves ...'

'It didn't last for Prochezka. Lots of Czechs lost money, thousands lost jobs. He vanished ...'

'And that was twenty-four years ago?' Wangley said.

'Yes.'

'Which means – either he's been in hiding somewhere for twenty-four years and has a skincare regime like no other, and suddenly died today. Or someone has paid to keep his body on ice for twenty-four years, for reasons known only to themselves. Neither story is at all satisfactory.'

'And a body kept "on ice", as you say, would not look like the one we saw today,' Marika said with frustration. 'That was not someone who's been dead for two decades ...'

Wangley agreed. 'It sounds to me that there might be some mysterious connection between Prochezka and those alchemists of old – who would sell their souls to find the truth behind the Philosopher's Stone ...'

'Perhaps this map you have will explain things to us,' she said.

'Of course,' Wangley said. 'The map. Another connection between the young Prochezka and the alchemists. They too left strange writings in code, some of which still cannot be translated hundreds of years later. For all we know, they might contain the recipes for elixirs – to give love, magical power or eternal life.'

'Are you suggesting Prochezka artificially prolonged his own life?' Marika asked, breathlessly.

'It's certainly starting to seem possible,' replied the earnest professor, in a decidedly serious tone. 'What a fascinating story, don't you think?'

'If a tad unnecessarily complicated and heavy on the exposition.'

Inwardly, Wangley demurred. He was used to going on feats of exposition that far exceeded this small speech. Enormous epics of it, indeed, agonisingly drawn out over many dozens of pages and chapters.

So – consider yourself lucky, is my point.

'As long as I can decode the map,' he said, 'we may have a chance of understanding what's going on and clearing our names. Perhaps we are now far enough away from the police to stop and try ...'

He halted and sat on a step. He took the map out, unfolded it and started murmuring to himself.

'This is ... hmm ...' He looked up. 'It's difficult. I can make out a word or two, as they've been written in cuneiform script. But they mean nothing to me ... They aren't in English. Could be in Czech, but I doubt it ...'

'Let's wait until we have a proper light source,' Marika agreed.

At that moment they heard echoing footsteps behind them, and Wangley turned his light off. From now on their progress would once more be through total darkness.

22

'These tunnels really do seem to go on forever,' Wangley said.

'They were flooded badly in 2002 and many of them abandoned. Some fell in,' said Marika. Then she gasped as her feet touched water. Wangley felt it too. He risked switching his light on for a moment.

Ahead of them the passage went downwards, and was entirely flooded.

Except, looking closely, they saw a narrow gap, barely a couple of centimetres, beneath the roof and the surface of the water (easy to miss at a first glance), which showed that further on the tunnel rose again.

Now there were lights behind them, and footsteps too. Coming closer every second.

'It's always been rumoured that this six-hundred-year-old tunnel goes under the river,' said Marika. 'But I never expected I could possibly discover the place where it happens. If I tried for a century I might never find it. If we swim through this tunnel, it will probably take us under the Vltava. And on the other side, a steep climb all the way to Prague Castle.'

The lights flashing on the walls got brighter, and the voices louder. Wangley looked fearfully at the water, but knew there was only one choice.

Less than a minute later, the authorities arrived, guns in hand and barking dogs straining on their leashes. They swept the space with their torches and saw only a faint ripple on the surface of the water.

They turned away, and continued searching ...

Yup, zero jokes in this chapter at all. Just plot.

23

Gustav Rulka ground his cigarette out on the floor, and, taking another one out of the packet, lit it. He blew a stream of blue smoke up into the air, which was brilliantly illuminated by the stark lights of the police lab.

All around him was the machinery of death: the harsh reflective metal of the tools, the sinister white tiles from which microbes and bodily fluids alike could be swabbed with ease.

Looking above all this gleaming equipment, Rulka's eyes met hard, cold stone. The hard, cold stone of a castle wall. The hard, stone castle wall of Prague Castle, which, despite being more than a thousand years old, was still the working heart of the country's government. A beating, pulsing heart. Unlike the hearts in this laboratory, which (with the exception of those belonging to Detective Rulka and the pathologist) were refrigerated, emptied of blood – and stone-cold dead.

The police laboratory had been moved inside the castle a few years earlier for ease of access to the state apparatus of law enforcement and intelligence agencies, which were already stationed there, and also to assist in a plot contrivance that will become clear in about two and a half pages' time.

'What was the cause of death?' Rulka asked.

'What *wasn't* the cause of death?' answered Dr Korac, the pathologist. 'I mean, look at this guy!'

'Otakar, please.'

'"Please," he says! It took me and three orderlies ten minutes to put the body together. Which piece went where? Left foot, right elbow ... I'll never play *Twister* again ...'

'Cause of death,' the cop repeated doggedly.

'His neck is broken, but so is everything else. His skull is crushed. By my guess, he was also tortured ...'

'We think he jumped from a window. Or was pushed ...' Rulka said gruffly.

'Look at these legs,' said Prague's leading criminal forensic pathologist. He held one of the victim's legs up by the trouser cuff. It was not stiff and straight, but as limp as a metal chain. He let go and the leg slithered back into place.

'The only thing he is jumping to is the conclusion his leg is broken in twelve places,' Korac said.

'You know what people are saying,' said Rulka, coming round to look the corpse in the face. He exhaled smoke into it.

'Yes, that this is the body of the famous boy who vanished,' said Korac. 'Witnesses at the scene, even the medic bringing him in. They all think it's him.'

'Even though it can't be — because this is a young man's body,' said Rulka. 'Must be a coincidence, that there's such a strong resemblance ...'

'But that's the thing,' said Korac. 'It *is* him. The DNA matches the one we have on file.' He handed over a report.

'Crazy!' said Rulka. 'Impossible! It does not seem at all possible! My credulity is under considerable strain right now!' He grabbed the results from Dr Korac, but could make neither head nor tail of them and threw them aside.

'Bialystock was the last link to the university,' said the esteemed pathologist. 'He was the last one working at the Experimental Physics Unit there. All the victims worked together – and now they're all dead.'

Rulka grunted. 'Seven people murdered over the course of a week. All working at the university, all hideously mutilated. Why none of them accepted our protection, I can't understand.'

'How will you find out their connection to the killer now?' Korac asked.

'There's a witness,' said Rulka. 'I'm just going to interrogate him. He claimed to have seen something impossible. A superhuman giant ...'

Korac gave the detective a slow, heavy-lidded look.

'Don't even suggest it,' Rulka said angrily. 'And you, a man of science! There are no magical creatures stalking the streets of Prague! No, I'm looking at Wangley, the American professor. His girlfriend vanishes from the room next to where the seventh victim, Bialystock, is being murdered. And just a few hours later, victim number eight is found and the professor is on the spot. No, too much of a coincidence, my friend ...'

'No professor did this,' said the pathologist. 'This man looks like he lost a fight with a trash compactor that had been really working out. And please don't tap ash into the victim's mouth like that, it plays havoc with my test results!' he added, handing him an ashtray.

'Come, Korac, you're looking like you will be sick again,' said Rulka. 'Let's get some fresh air in you. My god, you're too good a pathologist to give this up, though. Prague needs you …'

The two exited the lab, and their footsteps died away.

The room went silent.

Except for a little squeaking noise. Which slowly grew louder.

The castle walls had hidden doors and secret passageways within them. And behind one of these hidden entries, for the last few minutes, Wangley and Marika had been listening to the conversation as it unfolded.

'He really ought to change jobs,' said Wangley. 'It's terrible what it can do to you. Stress like that. My brother-in-law Hank, for example …'

'Richard, don't worry about that right now,' said Marika. 'Help me with this door.'

They both pushed. Millimetre by millimetre the gap widened, until with one final shove it was wide enough for them both to climb out. They stood wet, cold and shivering on the tiled laboratory floor.

'Seven other victims!' said Wangley. 'But that's crazy – they can't seriously suspect me, I only arrived in the country a few hours ago!'

'Here are their names,' said Marika, flicking through some of the doctor's notes. Wangley came and took a photo of the page with his phone. He was lucky it was still working. Swimming through the tunnel, he had just been able to hold it aloft so that it fitted through the gap between the stone roof above the edge of the water.

'Mencken, Kolesko, Kittling, Salz, Rabinowicz, Inuto,

Villalobos,' Wangley read. 'Not a particularly Czech list of individuals, unless I'm much mistaken.'

'And what links them,' said Marika, 'is working at the university.' She began reading their individual autopsy reports, while Richard used the bright laboratory lamp to look at the map again.

'It's …' he said. 'My god, it's fiendish!'

'You understand it?' Marika asked, glancing up.

'I think so, but – it's wild. Why write a message like this?'

'Like what?'

'Well, you see, the letters are cuneiform. And they – kind of, more or less – can be transliterated into Latin letters, or groups of them. If I do that, you see …'

Marika made a kind of disgusted grunt. 'No. It's still gibberish.'

'To most people yes, but this is ancient Akkadian. And I'm not fluent exactly, but I happen to have been studying it recently. The coincidence seems pretty crazy – even a tad suspicious.' The way his heart was beating told him that there was definitely something up. Could this message possibly have been meant for him, personally, out of all the people in Prague?

'So you can translate it?' she asked.

'I think so. Give me a minute … Yes. Listen to this. It says, "The answer to the mystery is in the ark, at the True Heart of Prague." Wow!'

Marika shook her head in amazement. She looked from the parchment to the esteemed secretismic symbology expert.

'Why do you think he wrote it?' she asked.

Wangley shrugged. 'And why stuff it in his mouth?' he asked. 'Cos he didn't want whoever was torturing him to read it, and he *did* want whoever found him to read it. But I've got one question ...'

'What's that?'

'I've met a few techies in my time. Even a few of the really famous ones. They're a type. They know what they know, and it's code. It's *not* ancient Akkadian ...'

'Richard,' Marika's arm clutched his. 'There's someone coming ...'

24

They knew that the castle complex was enormous and must have thousands of places to hide. But being unfamiliar with it, they had to turn back the way they had come and head for the tunnel.

Marika just managed to switch the lamp off and squeeze back into the tunnel, then pull the door closed in time. They huddled in darkness and peeped out through the narrow crack that was left.

In the room behind them they heard the squeak of many pairs of sneakers. No other noise.

Looking out, they glimpsed multiple lights flashing all around the room. Then a series of bulky shapes passed in front of their hiding places.

'Special forces,' whispered Marika.

Wangley saw she was right. Each wore combat gear and a head torch, and carried an automatic rifle raised and ready to fire.

'What are they doing here?' asked Richard.

'Let's talk about it later, when they've gone,' suggested Marika in the sublime suggestion of a micro-whisper.

He gave her a thumbs-up.

The agents swarmed the room, shining their lights and pointing their guns into every corner to establish it was empty.

Then, once they had communicated (via silent hand signals) that the room was secure, a leader entered and crossed to the dead body on the slab. He took his mask off, revealing a rock-like face, and above one of his expressionless eyes, a deep and deeply unpleasant star-shaped shrapnel scar. Which would be particularly helpful to identify him if he were going to appear again. But as it happens, he isn't.

He looked down at the pathologist's accumulated notes from all the dead bodies, flicked through them until he was satisfied these were the notes he was looking for.

Then, turning to the other soldiers, he indicated they had got what they wanted with a single word: '*Da.*'

Putting the mask on, he signalled for them to exit. And in two seconds they were gone from the room, accompanied only by the squeaking of their sneakers on the floor.

'They're Russian! What are Russian special forces doing here?' Marika asked.

'Yes. Either that or he's Irish and that was his father,' suggested Wangley. 'But your theory is probably more likely ...'

25

An hour, many miles of underground tunnel and a good deal more exposition later, Wangley and Marika tried another door, only to discover this time it was exactly what they had been looking for. It led out onto a main road rather than into a chamber in the heart of officialdom.

They quietly walked out, closing it after them as casually as if they were leaving their apartment. A few steps down the street, when they turned back to check no one was following them, they could not see any place along the blank stone wall where the door could have been.

'I need a chance to think,' said Wangley. 'And to sit down.'

'Here,' said Marika. She put her hand to the door of a building that to Wangley's eye looked firmly closed. The lights inside were dimmed to near-complete obscurity. Wangley glanced up at the sign sceptically.

'Caitriona O'Kelleher's,' said the sign, beside a picture of a pint of Guinness.

'I ought to have guessed,' said Wangley. 'An Irish pub.'

'Downstairs is one of the best jazz bars in Prague,' said Marika. 'It's very dark, we won't be spotted there.'

Wangley followed and soon found himself sitting in a cool stone chamber about the size of the average American water closet, in which eight jazz musicians were jammed on stage, jamming, while a crowd of four watched.

Wangley took his glass of lager beer and sat on a free table, next to a smiling curly-haired girl who was nodding along, absolutely wrapped up in the music, and her balding, dead-eyed, middle-aged companion.

As the agreeable noise washed over him and the first sip of beer entered his stomach, the professor started to try to arrange his thoughts.

'You heard what the cop and the doctor were talking about – what they were scared of?' he asked.

Marika, as a true Czech, knew the legend well. She gave him a grave look that communicated she knew exactly what he was referring to. A chilling legend that struck horror into the heart of every Prague citizen.

'It's a chilling legend that strikes horror into the heart of every Prague citizen,' she said. 'I'm no exception. It means you and I are cursed. And probably won't get out of this alive.'

Wangley nodded. He had feared it too.

'What's that?' he asked, looking at her glass.

'Sex on the Beach,' she said. 'Try it?'

'Um, no thanks. I'm good,' Wangley said.

Wangley had always adored jazz. It helped him think. The interplay of dissonance and consonance, the fiendish complexity, the brittle, improvisational style, layered and unresolved ...

It was inevitable that listening to such music, Wangley's thoughts drifted to Sir Clyffe Rycharde. The most famous of all the alchemists who ever lived in Prague, and said to be the most magically powerful person in the world. Although he died in 1610, he had made some eerie predictions. According to some, he had foretold the London plague of 1665 and the Great Fire that cleansed it. He had also predicted the rise of such people as Aleister Crowley, Adolf Hitler and Giles Brandreth.

He had travelled with an assistant, Matthew Kelley, who was said to have been a shape-shifter, capable of assuming many forms, and a keen astrologer. Contemporary accounts stated that he had the stars in his eyes.

Rycharde had taken many of his secrets to the grave — except for whatever was concealed within a famous grimoire, his spell book, which centuries later still defied translation. Wangley felt more and more that Prochezka and Rycharde were somehow linked.

They both sipped their drinks in a sombre mood. Finding she had finished hers, Marika went to order a Slippery Nipple.

But what is the link with Susannah? Wangley was asking himself. *Was Sir Clyffe Rycharde an original progenitor of Nometic Science? It was very possible. But how can I use this knowledge to help get her back?*

'Here,' said a man.

Richard realised he had been sitting on the man's coat. He stood up and the man took his place. Feeling awkward, Richard sat where the man had been sitting and (as the music began) realised he was on the piano.

It was too late to back out and important not to draw attention to themselves, so he decided to do his best to fit in. The other musicians watched as he implemented a rather staccato performance leaning deeply on the three years of lessons he'd had with old Mrs Kimblake in Butte, Michigan, ending when he was aged eight.

But, you know, he told himself – jazzy.

It was not quite like anything the other musicians had heard before. But this was a jam, after all. They listened, heads on their sides. Then, one by one, they joined in.

A tech genius making a Faustian pact ... Wangley thought.

A sequence of horrific murders of citizens apparently connected to the Experimental Physics Unit at the university ...

Susannah was due to give a world-changing talk tonight, revealing the untapped truth of the human mind ... Who wanted her silenced?

The Philosopher's Stone ... And we may be being chased by that ancient magical creature of Prague ...

He suddenly knew what they must do. He finished his set with a flourish and unexpectedly received a round of applause. He rode the applause, stood up and swayed his hips, played a few chords with his left ankle, then a few more with his buttocks, and, taking Marika by the hand, had her out on the street in a trice.

'Richard?' she asked. 'You hardly had a chance to sample your Pilsner!'

'We must go,' he said. 'I know where the heart of Prague is!'

26

Detective Rulka offered a cigarette to the witness, who took it with shaking fingers.

'Tell me again what you saw,' he said.

The witness was a young man of twenty-five, with long, lank hair and an open shirt. He looked harassed, afraid.

'It was this huge person — bigger than I've ever seen — maybe eight, nine foot tall ... truly massive ...' said the man.

Rulka grabbed his hair and smashed the man's face against the table.

'It's impossible!' he yelled. 'You're lying to me!'

'I'm not!' said the witness. 'I swear it's the truth!'

'There are no monsters in Prague, no supernatural beings!' Rulka insisted. 'You're on drugs. Who sold you the drugs?'

'I'm on antihistamines for hay fever,' said the witness.

'Forget it,' said Rulka. He went and sat opposite the witness, then pushed a bunch of pictures over the table to him. 'Look at these. Let me know if you recognise anyone.'

The young man shook his head as he leafed through them. A comingled droplet of sweat and tears hung on the tip of his nose.

He pointed a trembling finger at one of the pictures.

'This person? You've seen them?'

'It's Beyoncé Knowles,' said the witness. He shrank back in the chair as Rulka leaned over the table to take a closer look at the pictures.

'And this one ...' said the witness nervously, 'I'm pretty sure is Timothée Chalamet.'

'Timothée *who?*' barked Rulka. 'I could have sworn that was a young Sigourney Weaver.'

'Chalamet,' said the witness, more confident. 'He was in *Dune.*'

'I got you a Vodka Coke,' said Dr Korac, returning to the table from the bar. 'Come on, we've got to get our picture round handed in before the quiz starts.'

'I'm starting to think,' Rulka growled, a light of realisation coming into his eyes, 'that it's irresponsible of us to go to a pub quiz when there are so many crimes happening in the city tonight.'

'I was kind of thinking the same thing myself,' admitted Dr Korac. 'There could be another crime scene to attend at any minute. We should go back to the station.'

'Can I go now?' asked the witness.

'Quiet, you!' roared Rulka, grabbing his head and pounding it repeatedly into the table. As he did so he took on a reflective expression. The rhythmic exercise helped him think.

27

The doors of the National Museum of Art were closed. It was after 11 p.m. as they reached it.

Richard rapped sharply on the door to wake a sleeping security guard. Once roused, he came forward to the window and peered out sceptically.

'Quickly!' shouted Richard. 'This is very important!'

The guard sleepily indicated that they should go to the side of the building where a door might be unlocked.

Soon afterwards he was speaking to them over an intercom. Marika translated Richard's words, which were blunt and forceful. Had not the guard heard? There had been a terrible series of museum break-ins through the night. They told him to turn the news on if he wanted to check. Richard was, they explained, the curator of the Smithsonian Museum in Washington, and they currently had an invaluable work on loan here. Richard was demanding to see it, to satisfy himself it was safe.

The guard was gradually and reluctantly worn down, and at last unlocked the door. He saw how physically unthreatening the guests were and also felt sorry that they appeared to be shivering from the wet and the cold. (He was unaware that it had not rained that night. From their appearance, having emerged from the underground tunnels, he would have supposed there had been a deluge.)

At last he led them to the Grand Hall, and left them to satisfy themselves that the artwork was unharmed. He then withdrew, muttering to himself about vandals and how they ought to be shot, forced to do military service, beaten to within an inch of their lives. Preferably in that order.

'Here it is ...' said Wangley. 'Why did I not think of it before? The heart of Prague!'

Above them was the giant 1645 canvas of the painting *Prague Heart* by Seraglio Caravannio.

'The map seems to imply that there's a message hidden in the centre of this canvas,' Wangley said. They looked. On the left side was the river, and on the right were two armies clashing amid much smoke, fire and explosion. The river was even tainted red by the blood flowing from the battlefield.

However, in the very centre of the painting was a detail not normally noticed by most: a boat on the river, perhaps at first glance a supply vessel for one of the armies. But on closer inspection it wasn't rendered in the contemporary style. It seemed out of place, and out of time.

'One might almost say ... it was a biblical ark ...' Wangley muttered wonderingly.

'Yes!' Marika said, clapping her hands. 'You're right! My god!'

Richard had already fetched a step-ladder from where it was leaning in a corner and climbed it to inspect the surface of the painting.

'I can't see anything,' he said. He scanned it with an infrared pen he carried in his pocket, which was miraculously undamaged by immersion in water. 'No message, nothing added to the surface of the painting.'

'Perhaps it's behind?' said Marika.

Wangley climbed back down the ladder and examined the painting from further back. The magnificent frame (a present from Denmark's King Arnald in 1811) was historical itself, made of walnut coated in silver leaf, weighing over a tonne and a half, and stupendously expensive. The painting itself was thirty feet wide and ten tall.

'Well,' he said, 'we're not going to find out just by looking at it.'

It was two minutes' work to find a second ladder and for each of them to climb up to try to examine both ends of the enormous painting.

'It says here, "EXTREME DANGER DO NOT TOUCH",' said Marika.

'I think I've got it,' said Wangley. 'There's something behind here, I'm sure of it ...'

'"This painting must not be touched by anyone except the licensed hangers. This is VERY SENSITIVE and could fall EASILY." I'm not sure about this, Richard ...'

'Just ... here ... yes, there's something ... ah.'

There was a snapping sound, then a moment's silence that seemed to have the same weight as an avalanche, followed by the most thunderous crash Marika had ever heard.

28

Marika and Richard reached the safety of a doorway on the other side of the street as a phalanx of police cars came screeching to a halt in front of the National Museum, sirens blaring. Officers poured out of their cars and towards the front door.

'There was nothing there?' Marika asked incredulously.

'I'm afraid not. I just had time to examine the canvas closely — what was left of it,' Richard said. 'It's most irresponsible of them to have hung it directly in front of the famous *Dance of the Hundred Bronze Swords* sculpture.'

'Sliced to ribbons,' said Marika, closing her eyes. 'Our national treasure.'

'Most unfortunate,' said Richard stiffly.

'And that poor security guard,' Marika breathed. The frail-looking man was already being led away in handcuffs and manhandled into a patrol car.

'It is certainly a shame,' Richard conceded. 'He is the latest casualty of the heartless tactics being employed by whoever is trying to set us up ...'

Marika let out a sigh of profound exhaustion. It had been a long night.

When they had told the security guard of the three earlier break-ins, they'd not been lying. Marika and Richard were of course far from professional burglars. But necessity is the mother of invention, and when so much was at stake, extreme methods were called for.

Three break-ins, three paintings examined, three terrible accidents. Masterpieces by Viennetta, Ristretto and Kantuchdis, all destroyed.

And not one had yielded an answer to the mystery.

Such a trail of destruction wrought by a few words scribbled on a piece of paper in just a few hours! Marika was starting to feel uncomfortable about her involvement in the expedition.

But one must not look back. There were lives to save.

'Do you have any other ideas, Richard? What do we do next?'

'Yes, I suddenly realised when I saw the shredded remains of the painting, that there is somewhere else we ought to have been looking ... The true *heart of Prague* ... It was there on the map all along ...'

Keeping to the shadows and side streets, they crossed the centre of the city until they were standing in front of the statue of Jan Hus, religious renegade, protester against the corruption of the Roman Catholic Church, proto-Protestant and leader of the Hussite Revolution. In many ways he had symbolised the emotional heart of the Czech nation, and Wangley was now sure that *this* was what was meant by the message.

The statue was in the middle of a square that was not square at all. 'Look at the map,' he said. In the street plan one could see that the square was in fact heart-shaped. 'And look at the name of the square. Arkada Square. *Arkada* means "ark"! The ark in the heart of Prague!'

Marika gasped. 'You're amazing, Richard,' she said. 'It must be here. But where will the message be hidden?'

'Somewhere in or near this statue,' said Wangley. 'Possibly in his pocket or about his chest area. We just have to find a way of reading it ...'

Marika stared up in amazement. No wonder the professor kept finding himself in the centre of international intrigues involving the art world. He was a genius at interpreting clues and finding out to what they referred. She just hoped that this statue (which she had always admired) would not have to suffer in the service of their investigation ...

Her attention was arrested by a beep-beep-beep, and she turned to find that Richard had hot-wired a cherry-picker and manoeuvred it into place by the statue's head. Also, somehow he had laid his hands on a sledgehammer, which he was now wielding with every ounce of strength he had.

'Richard! Where did you get that? Look out! Be careful!'

There was a deep clonk, and the head rolled off the statue and landed on the pavement in a shower of gritty fragments.

'Richard! I must insist!' she yelled as another blow shattered the statue's shoulder.

'Perhaps I'll have better luck if I went for the legs ...' she heard Richard saying to himself.

'Please! Professor Wangley! Show some respect! I beg of you!'

There were two more loud cronks, and then the statue started listing to starboard, and eventually came down onto the pavement with a tremendous groan and smash. Windows were lighting up in the buildings around as Wangley excitedly hopped down from the machine and began a close examination.

He tutted and sighed, searched every inch of the stonework, and started to grow frustrated.

'I can't see anything!' he said.

'Richard, you've destroyed this beloved artefact!' Marika wailed.

Suddenly they both became aware that for the past minute or so sirens had been coming closer and closer. Now flashing blue lights appeared simultaneously both ahead of and behind them.

'We must go!' said Marika. 'Now!'

Richard dropped the sledgehammer and joined her, hiding behind a hedge at an apartment building opposite.

'Just look at it!' said Richard, reviewing the damage with utter dismay. 'These villains will stop at nothing to get what they want …'

'What chance do we have now?' Marika lamented. 'The police will surely catch us. After all, the Czech police are notoriously diligent, hardworking and insightful …'

29

Detective Rulka paced up and down the corridor. Around him were the noises of office life, which bounced against his ears like cascading water over a waterfall – onto hard ice. Ice that was starting to fragment under the pressure, showing signs of being about to crack.

He punched the wall in frustration.

From a nearby office Detective Svobodnik wandered out. He was bald and overweight, with sweat patches under his armpits and bags under his bloodshot eyes. A moustache drooped over his top lip, giving him a mournful expression, and he was temporarily incapacitated by a coughing fit.

He gestured for Rulka to join him in the office, then sagged heavily into his chair, which creaked beneath him. At the age of twenty-three, he was the freshest recruit in the force.

'What's eating you, Rulka?' he said, with a voice like gravel being scrunched under the wheels of a fuel-injected Skoda Santaris four-wheel drive with optional tinted windows, Bluetooth dash cam and portable tyre pressure gauge.

'It's Dr Korac,' Rulka said. 'I just forced him to take a sedative. Try and close his eyes for an hour. The guy's in pieces.

Goddammit, this case is killing him. He's the best pathologist this city's ever had ...'

'You're a good friend to that man,' said Svobodnik. 'But you've got to think about yourself. And that's why I wanted to see you. You know I've got to make sure our detectives are looking after themselves.'

'I know it,' said Rulka, avoiding the other man's eye.

'We're protecting the people here, for god's sake,' Svobodnik said. 'We owe it to them to make sure we're in good shape.'

Rulka nodded, reluctantly.

Svobodnik fixed him with a stern, unwavering glance. 'You know what I'm going to ask. How's the drinking?'

'I've been trying hard,' said Rulka. 'You know how I struggle.'

'Tell me,' insisted Svobodnik. 'Be honest.'

'I'm drinking about a bottle of vodka a day.'

'And cigarettes?'

'Forty a day, maybe.'

The other man sighed. All the energy seemed to go out of him and he ran a trembling hand over his face. He was clearly shocked.

'I'm trying. God knows I'm trying,' said Rulka. Although he was a tough guy, a bull of a man, with a bear's hide and the heart of a lion, a pleading note entered his voice. Like a rebuked spaniel, or more accurately, a human man begging to be understood by a valued colleague.

'I'll do better,' Rulka said.

'I know you can,' said Svobodnik. 'This department has protocols. I have to report this, unless I can be sure you will ...'

'I *will*,' Rulka insisted. Now he was speaking with the confidence of a polar bear and the rugged integrity of a beluga whale.

'Okay,' said the other. 'I want to see you up to two bottles a day by the end of the week. And three packs of cigarettes, minimum.'

'I won't let you down,' said Rulka.

'This city is depending on you,' Svobodnik replied. 'Now get out there and catch this murderer.'

30

Richard and Marika had retreated to the welcome anonymity of the narrow backstreets. Sirens blared ahead of them and behind, as the police tried to get to grips with what must seem to them a bewildering crime wave.

It felt like officers might come rushing down the alley at any moment, guns drawn (that was, Richard reflected, if Czech officers had guns – for all he knew, they might use cudgels or bows and arrows).

'Look, a fire escape,' said Marika.

'Well spotted,' said Richard. He climbed swiftly and leaned down to help Marika behind him. In moments they were up and out of sight of anyone on street level.

Seeing that a nearby window was open, they looked in to see if it might be a safe hiding place.

It was a bedroom in what appeared to be an apartment. A large, strong-looking man with a mournful expression was sitting on a bed talking into a handset.

'I don't know what you want, I don't know who you are,' he was saying threateningly in an Irish accent. 'But you have crossed the wrong person. I've got a very particular set of skills. And if you don't return what belongs to me, I *will* hunt you, and I *will* kill you ...'

As he spoke his voice became deeper and more intense. His body shook with rage, the muscles across his shoulders tightened, his eyes became as hard as bricks and as black as coals that are not on fire. He started to shake with menace and power like a volcano in the early to middle stage of the beginning of a major eruption.

So in thrall to his emotions was this man, in fact, that his thumb slipped over the speakerphone button.

'... our employees deserve to be spoken to respectfully and will report any instances of abuse ... your call *is* important to us and will be answered shortly ... all calls are recorded for monitoring purposes ...'

The man straightened his back and looked to the ceiling, as though unable to contain his fury.

'... thank you for calling easyJet,' the voice went on. 'Your position in the queue is ... ninety ... four ...'

'Let's get back down the fire escape,' whispered Marika.

'Yes,' agreed Richard. 'Before there's a third Defenestration of Prague. I think I'd feel safer with the police anyway, at this rate ...'

31

The being who knew its name was Alphonso Emmettio was trembling with emotion.

Things had changed.

It had been a busy evening.

There were tasks to perform, ordained by its master. It had performed many of them in the past few days.

There had been eight names now, on the list. The people Alphonso had to go to, and about whom afterwards he could remember nothing.

But there had been something else as well. Something important.

In order to complete his tasks, Alphonso must not get caught. He had to understand these strange people of the city.

He watched them, and the more he watched, the more he wanted to learn.

People did not just walk to and fro, and eat and sleep. They did other things for no obvious reason.

He walked along by the river for no reason. He saw others doing that. In the river were fish that might be nice to eat.

In the air were birds it might also be nice to eat. He watched the people throw food to the ducks – giving food away, to other food.

It would be going too far to say he was fascinated. He simply watched. He did not understand. But if he kept watching, perhaps he would understand.

His extremely rudimentary reading skills were gradually (under force of necessity) improving. 'All You Can Eat' said a sign in a restaurant. He went there and had a satisfying meal. It took some time.

The next day, he walked that way again. The restaurant didn't seem to be there any more.

Then he went to a bookshop.

The bookseller, a slim old lady with glasses and sharp brown eyes, looked at him carefully. She regarded him as a challenge. She liked a challenge. As he stood there with his head hair brushing against the ceiling tiles, she quizzed him. And then sent him away with a book in his hand.

The book was called *The Power of Now*.

Now here he was in his bedroom, lying in the cone of light from his bedroom lamp and reading it.

In the room, nothing was moving except the occasion leaf of paper.

In his mind, nothing was still.

He must fit in, so he could continue carrying out his deeds. Reading this book was therefore also one of his deeds.

He turned another page.

32

The streets were now heavily patrolled by law enforcement. With such a number of serious incidents recorded in a single evening, the city was under high alert, and police vehicles were crawling up and down every thoroughfare.

'We need to get somewhere quiet,' said Wangley. 'I feel this code was left for me, and I'm sure I'm going to crack it soon. I just need a chance to think …'

'We have to change our appearances,' said Marika. 'By now we're bound to have been picked up by CCTV. The footage will be analysed sooner or later and then they'll have our descriptions.'

'Excuse me, sir!' said Wangley. A few yards away, an elderly gentleman was locking the door to his shopfront. He looked up, surprised at being addressed.

'May I help you?' he asked.

'I see you are closing your fancy dress emporium,' said Wangley. 'May we prevail on you to open the business for a few more minutes?'

'I stay open late once a month,' the man admitted. 'But business tonight has been deadly …'

It's not the only thing in this city that's deadly, thought Wangley. *Not by a long shot ...*

He took out his wallet and handed a sizeable sum to the shop owner, as a gesture of good will.

'Business is looking up,' said the man, taking out his keys again.

A few short minutes (and a lot of Czech koruna) later, Marika and Wangley were back out on the street.

'Hopefully now the police won't take a second look at us,' said Wangley. 'It's essential that we remain inconspicuous. The last thing we want to do is draw attention to ourselves.'

'We know that the police have our descriptions,' said Marika. 'They definitely won't be looking for a Mexican bandit and someone in a devil costume.' She twirled her devil's tail with satisfaction.

'Thank god,' said Richard. 'Now we can blend in ...'

33

Soon they were ensconced at the quietest, most invisible table at the back of a late-night restaurant. Marika ordered food while Richard looked at the map again.

'Let's look at what we know,' he said. 'Someone or something dropped this man, who has not been seen for twenty-four years, from the sky. What do you think it means?'

'You think it has something to do with Faust,' she replied.

'Yes and no. The real Faust was a magician and an astrologer. But he was also in the business of *dispelling* myths and magic. That's why the story of his soul being taken by the devil was put about by the Catholic Church. He claimed he could replicate all the miracles of Christ, just to show they were tricks any clever mortal could perform. And when he went to Venice, rumour had it he tried to fly, and fell from the sky.'

'The author is displaying his needless research again,' said Marika desperately. 'There hasn't been a joke for the last ten lines, for god's sake!'

'*He can't write a holiday in Prague off for tax unless it goes in,*' said Wangley urgently, leaning in close. Stress written in his every feature, a vein pulsing at his temple.

'Fine, just get it over with quickly then,' replied Marika, with equal intensity, her brown eyes as wide, deep and intense as bowls of traditional beef *svíčkova* stew.

Her particular choice of words reminded Richard of time spent in the bedroom (*her* bedroom) with his darling Susannah, and he felt a pang at her loss.

'Then there's the elephant in the room,' he went on, forcing the thought from him with a dismissive shudder, which was also in its own way reminiscent of his girlfriend. 'The Golem.'

It was the first time either of them had mentioned the creature by name, and at the acknowledgement of this dark foe, their eyes locked together in an iron embrace of despair.

'The monster crafted from mud,' said Marika.

'A man-shaped creature from Jewish mythology, called forth by the rabbi at times of need, which cannot be stopped by any force on earth …'

'… except its master's voice,' said Marika.

'It will kill without qualm or conscience. And remember,' said Richard, turning to the map again, 'the Golem was given its instructions on a parchment placed *inside its mouth* …'

Marika shook her head. 'What do you think it all means?'

'I think someone wants us to solve this mystery and find what the map is pointing to – which is something that must not fall into the wrong hands. At first glance, it feels like Prochezka sold his soul, had his good fortune – and then his luck ran out. The devil came to collect on the deal. But during his years of experimentation and technical innovation, he found something. Something, if not magical, then immensely powerful …'

Marika was staring at him. 'The Philosopher's Stone?'

Richard gulped. He hadn't intended it to be spoken out loud, because it sounded sort of stupid.

'You think this is what has happened?' she persevered.

The professor shook his head. 'Who can tell? But there sure are a lot of meaningful coincidences here, pointing that way. I think someone's playing with our heads.'

'Me too,' said Marika. She looked out of the window across the street. From her vantage point, she could see clearly a hundred yards down one of the many narrow alleys in Prague's Old Town. And as she looked, a huge shape – no, an *enormous* shape – passed across the alley. Larger than any human being she had ever seen in the flesh. Terrifyingly big, and moving with a steady, unhurried tread. Almost like it was sleepwalking.

As it passed, great swirls of mist spun in its wake.

34

Marika shuddered violently and looked round, to see that Richard had been following her glance. She thought she'd seen him react too, but he was refusing to meet her eye.

'These other words at the bottom of the map,' said Richard, 'I didn't notice them before. They're much more rushed, and harder to translate. The sense is garbled. It says, "Secrets of …"' He frowned. 'It's bad grammar. It says something like, "Secretest of secretisms".'

'Okay, what does that make you think of?' she asked.

Richard thought. 'My mind goes to the "Secret of secrets", a medieval text that purported to be a document written by Aristotle for his pupil, Alexander the Great.'

'What was in it?' Marika asked.

'Lore – scientific knowledge. Secrets, naturally. Alchemical mysteries, how to locate the Philosopher's Stone and so on. The English magician Sir Clyffe Rycharde, who lived in Prague, had a copy. It was guessed that the document was intended to give one the power to take over the world. Conquer the spiritual and metaphysical world, just as he already had dominated the world geographically. To become a god, I guess …'

'Alchemy again,' Marika said. 'We keep coming back to it.'

'But importantly, the *Secret of Secrets* was itself a fake – a pretend text written by medieval Islamic scribes in Baghdad in perhaps the ninth century. And another thing we should remember,' Richard explained, 'is that alchemy is not really about making gold. It's not a ticket to wealth or a way of upscaling any base metals you have to hand.'

'No?'

'Not really. It's a metaphor. It's about turning oneself into something better. Finding a way to transform. To break through into another way of being. It's spiritual …'

'I have to admit, Richard,' Marika said, 'I've never quite known what a metaphor is.'

'A metaphor …' Richard thought for a moment, trying to dream up a good example. 'Well, language is a stony garden full of straggling weeds, and a metaphor is the flower that blooms unexpectedly from such unfruitful ground.'

Marika nodded thoughtfully.

'And how about the Philosopher's Stone?' she asked. 'I've often wondered what that is. It's something you find, or something you use …?'

'Again. A metaphor. It might be a stone, or a powder, or an elixir. Or a song, or a spell … It's just the means by which a powerful sorcerer – these days we would say scientist – would exercise their power over the physical realm.'

'Like Gandalf's staff?' Marika said. 'Or Austin Powers's mojo?'

'A certain *je ne sais quoi*,' Richard agreed. 'An ineffable magical quality.'

'And not a stone.'

'Who knows? But probably not. No.'

She nodded thoughtfully again, and gazed at other couples tucking into their food. Chatting and laughing as though nothing important was going on.

'Wait,' said Richard. 'I think I've got it. *The heart of Prague...*'

He held up the map, and pointed to the very centre. It was only when he held it up against the light that they saw a detail which had escaped them earlier. There was a distinct hole in the very centre of the map, as though punched there by the thrust of a pen nib in order to draw attention to this precise point.

'My goodness,' said Marika, leaning forward. 'I can't believe we didn't see it before!'

'We must get there at once, before anyone else,' said Richard. 'We have to prove our innocence once and for all, and get those cops off our trail. I mean, my god! That they could seriously think me responsible. An American university professor coming to Europe incognito, to commit a series of gruesome, bloody murders...?' He laughed bitterly. 'It's unbelievable.'

'I've got two portions of goulash,' said a waiter, sidling up to the table, adroitly balancing a number of plates.

'We'll have those to go,' said Marika. 'And the bill.'

'No problem,' said the waiter. He moved smoothly to the next table, where a customer was half-hidden behind the wing of an armchair.

'And I've got a glass of chianti,' he said, placing it on the table, 'and fava beans with liver. Plus a side of...' he squinted at the dish in his hand, and said quietly to himself, '... I didn't know we served that...'

The customer inhaled with relish, making a wet, sibilant, lip-smacking sound. Everyone who was sat in earshot felt a sudden uncontrollable shiver.

35

The day after his realisation that Life was for Living, Alphonso went to a golf club. He tried hitting a ball under the supervision of a tutor, but after he swung the club, the ball didn't exist any more. There was just a fine white dust in the breeze. He was politely asked to leave.

He went to the cinema and sat in the front row. He watched a film about an enormous shadow that didn't move, while some colours shifted around in the rest of the screen. None of the other patrons seemed to enjoy it either.

The Performance Water-Skiing Team he approached had a policy of never turning anyone down. And besides, he looked so extraordinary that any water-ski pyramid with him in it would be equally eye-catching.

And during practice, when they were all performing at top performance level, there was an electric signal that went through his brain. *I am alive*, it thought. *This is what it is like to be alive*.

Then there was the pottery class. Alphonso went to the door and peered in.

At the back of the class was a Female. A very tall Female,

of extraordinary bulk. With a very open expression. And whose eyes met his.

'Are you coming in?' asked the woman running the class.

He manoeuvred awkwardly to the back of the class, blushing. And sat. At the next potter's wheel to the Female.

Shyly, she turned and smiled at him.

He smiled back.

She smiled back.

He smiled back.

36

'I can't believe it,' said Richard, peeping out from a doorway. He looked back down at the map and showed it to Marika.

'It's definitely the spot,' she said dubiously. 'I mean, there's nothing else on this street ...'

Richard sighed. 'Well, we'd better brave it,' he said.

They paused while a police car rolled by and let their breath out once it turned a corner. Then they broke cover and crossed to the open door, above which was a brightly flashing pink neon sign.

'Welcome!' drawled the person at the door, whose speech was blurred by the twenty or thirty piercings in and around their mouth. 'Please come in. You are just in time for Whiplash night. You are members?'

Richard gulped.

'Our friend told us to come,' said Marika firmly. 'We're meeting him inside.'

'I'm afraid your costumes – charming as they are – are not appropriate. Your friend did not tell you about this?'

'He was fuzzy about the details,' said Richard. 'Are you

sure you can't let us in?' He handed over enough notes to pay for entry.

'Ah,' said their host, into one of whose dozens of zipped pockets the money disappeared instantaneously, and with apparent finality. 'We have a strict dress code for our special nights. You must comply to enter …'

'Don't you have a lost property closet or something?' Richard asked, before he'd had a chance to think. 'We have to come in.'

The host regarded him drolly, gave him a lengthy look up and down, before nodding. With the hint of a smirk.

'I think I've got something that would suit you perfectly …' he said.

A few minutes earlier, when the two of them had reached the corner of the street and set eyes on the establishment they were about to enter, Marika had expressed doubts. But Wangley was sure.

'This is definitely it!' he'd said. 'Don't you see?'

'I don't see why someone in the process of being tortured to death would direct us to a sex dungeon, no, Richard,' Marika had replied. 'I admit it.'

'But it's so obvious,' he'd said. '"The heart of Prague". The city grew up at a bend in the Vltava River, where the river was shallow and could be crossed by horse. The word "Prague" means "shoal" or "threshold". Look!'

Marika had looked. The club's neon title, PAIN THRESHOLD, pulsed in the night.

'Where better to hide whatever it was he had to hide?' Richard had said. 'This secret, or hidden treasure, this key to the mystery …'

Marika had nodded reluctantly, while giving the middle-aged professor a slow, evaluating look as though he might be mad, or brilliant. Or slightly kinky.

(He wasn't.)

The host came forth from the back office with some costumes and then directed the two of them to the bathrooms. When Richard came out, he was distinctly uncomfortable.

'Well,' said Marika. 'It's a statement.'

'What about you?' Wangley asked. 'You haven't changed!'

'They said I'm okay as I am, as long as I wear this mask.'

'Gosh darn it – pardon my language – it took me ages to get into this thing,' said Richard. 'And the PVC is agony – it really irritates my rosacea!'

'We must all make sacrifices. Remember you are trying to clear your name. Isn't your, um, your *derrière* a little cold?'

'It does feel the draught,' admitted the world-famous symbologistical secretismist.

'*Avanti*,' said Marika.

'If you're ready, follow me!' said their host, pushing open a swing door. From within escaped a gust of warm, damp air and the sound of whips landing on human flesh.

37

'But our lives depend on staying inside!' insisted an outraged Professor Wangley, twenty minutes later, as he was escorted to the pavement.

'I'm sorry,' said the host dispassionately, 'but the night is open only to those who are willing to participate. I must request that you do not try to enter the premises again. This is a private club that caters to a special clientele and our members are offended by people trying to enter under false pretences.'

'Our clothes!' Richard shouted at the door, which was now firmly shut.

'That was unfortunate,' Marika admitted. 'But I've got to say you lasted longer than I expected ...'

'How could the night get any worse?' Richard wondered aloud. 'At least if I get arrested for murder there's a chance to clear my name, and my ass won't be this cold ...'

'We're attracting attention,' Marika concluded, looking up and down the street. It was now well past midnight, and the number of pedestrians had increased. They also appeared to rove in groups and to be under the influence of alcohol.

Which in itself was not necessarily a problem, especially in a modern, European and sex-positive city centre. But beyond the droves of police, the Russian special forces and the secret murderer who was abroad in the darkness of the Czech nightscape, there was another more immediate and toxic threat: the British stag party group.

These gatherings of men tended not to be entirely up to date on sexual politics and political correctness, or even general manners and deportment. They had seen many such groups during their voyages across the city, and the idea of running into one of them now made Richard feel an icy chill almost as stark as the one that was currently assaulting his nether portions.

'Let's walk,' he agreed.

'Maybe there is no answer to the mystery,' said Marika despairingly, as they turned down a narrow alley. 'Maybe it was the desperate ravings of a frightened man. Maybe he wrote the wrong words.'

'Don't give in to that sort of thinking,' said Richard. 'We have to keep trying to understand this maze we are in ...'

'You're right. Do you want my wig to help cover your backside?'

'Kind of you,' he replied. 'But I feel that would make me look even more bizarre. Like some kind of BDSM baboon.' They turned left, then right, then left, losing themselves in the narrow alleyways between the tall Baroque apartment buildings of the mystical city. The night closed in around them, and at every turn they expected to be confronted by someone with a gun and an arrest warrant.

They were weary, demoralised, growing paranoid. They began to think all was lost. Worse, because they were not following a specific route, they started to fear they were going in circles. They were out of ideas.

'I wonder if you're right,' said Richard huskily. It felt like their cause was lost. He was about to suggest that she abandon him and try to save herself. 'We may never find out what is …' he began.

At that moment the alleyway they were traversing turned an angle and ahead of them a brightly lit building came into view.

He didn't finish his sentence. The name on the sign did it for him.

'The Heart O'Prague', proclaimed the sign. 'Formerly Siobhain O'Suillaibhain's', it said in smaller writing underneath. And then in huge capitals: 'AN IRISH PUB.'

38

There are Irish pubs, and there are Irish pubs.

There are, to be more precise, ersatz Celtic drinking establishments that boast only the Guinness emblem and English-language signage, and otherwise conform to local traditions in their presentation and habits.

This was not such a one. The Heart O'Prague (formerly Siobhain O'Suillaibhain's) was, by happenstance, an *Irish* pub. The clientele were bulky, balding, past middle age and clustered on stools around heavy wooden tables, where they maintained a quiet, rumbling conversation. And that included the women.

Old photographs of Ireland (featuring carts, shawls, large puddles and spectacular mountains in sepia) decorated the walls.

Drinkers kept to themselves and nobody showed the slightest interest in newcomers. The lighting was dim and forgiving, for which at this particular time more than ever, Professor Richard Wangley was especially grateful.

'Two pints of Guinness, please,' said Marika.

The barman, a self-contained bearded fellow, nodded and

began to pour. He glanced at them both with mild, friendly curiosity.

'This might seem like a strange question,' said Richard. 'But does the phrase "secretest of secretisms" mean anything to you?'

The barman watched the pint of stout he was pouring, as it filled. He focused on the glass absolutely, appearing totally engrossed in his task.

'Prochezka sent you?' he asked quietly, in an even voice.

'Yes,' said Richard, struggling to keep his voice calm.

'Sure, I've something for you,' said the barman. He put one glass aside, then took another and set it pouring. Then he turned around and looked up at a little shelf above the till, between the bottles of spirits. There were a couple of books about beer, a faded photo of a former publican, a few pieces of currency pinned to the shelf edges, presumably counterfeit. In the middle, between all these things, however, was what looked like a child's toy: a wooden model of Noah's Ark.

He lifted the lid with one hand and reached inside with the other. Marika and Richard exchanged a stunned look.

The barman turned back round and dropped an envelope on the bar, then stopped the Guinness to let it settle. Just as they do in Ireland, Richard noted: not halfway up, but when the glass was just millimetres short of being full.

'I'll bring your drinks over,' he said. 'You sit yourselves down.'

As they sat on the carpet-upholstered stools around a small circular table, Richard held up what they had been given. It was just an ordinary-sized white envelope. As plain as could be, except that on the outside was handwritten "secretest of secretisms". It had hardly any weight, no bulge from anything inside.

'Open it,' said Marika.

Almost afraid lest he might damage the contents, his trembling fingers peeled back the flap. When open, he held it forward so she could see inside as well as he could. Within was just a slip of paper.

'You take it,' he said.

Marika pulled out the slip between forefinger and thumb. Then put it on the table for both of them to see.

'Oh no,' Marika clutched her forehead.

'Another code,' sighed the well-known professor.

39

The code on the page in front of them was, at least, shorter than the previous one they'd faced. It was just eight letters long. This time the letters were in another script Marika couldn't recognise.

'Ancient Celtic,' said Richard, anticipating her question. 'And once I've translated it into Roman script, I bet it will need translating again before we can understand it ...'

'Why would he do this?' Marika asked, exasperated. 'What is his plan?'

'I'm starting to wonder ...' said Richard, a faraway look in his eyes.

He copied the letters onto a napkin to translate them later – the envelope and the paper were of course evidence. Not having a pocket to place them in for safekeeping, he tucked them inside the cleavage of his costume.

Then, after puzzling over the letters for a few moments, he looked up.

'Have you still got your phone on you?' he asked.

She nodded.

'Good,' he said. 'Of course, keeping it is a risk in case they track you, but it's one worth taking. The police would have to know your identity in order to trace your phone, and I'm guessing you're not already known to the Czech authorities?'

'Of course not,' she bristled.

'In which case, can I look something up on your browser?'

She willingly handed her phone over, and unlocked it for him.

'I just recalled the old friend I was supposed to meet earlier,' Richard explained. 'Not only will he be worried about me, but in a pinch he might be someone we can turn to for clothes and a chance to gather our thoughts …'

He sat up straight on his stool. 'My god!' he exclaimed. 'It can't be!' He slumped back, looking exhausted and defeated, and without looking at her, handed the phone back with a limp hand.

'What is it?' she asked. She glanced at the screen.

'It gets worse and worse,' said Richard. 'I can feel the net closing in around me. That is one of my oldest friends. The only person I know in Prague. I received a message from him this evening inviting me to meet him. At the bar where I saw you. Now I see this – it says JAROSLAV SEDLAK, RIP. Whoever's behind this must have known about me being in Prague and been setting me up from the start. Why? *And how …?*'

'But Richard,' the physically attractive and emotionally strong woman said to him in reply. 'There's nothing wrong here.'

'How can you say that?' he replied, aghast. 'The man is dead!'

'That is not what this says,' she replied, unfazed. 'He appears to be quite well, as far as I can tell.'

'Can't you see?' protested the North American academic. 'There's his name, with the letters "RIP" beside it!'

'Richard, please stop acting like a character in a badly written novel who refuses to pick up on glaringly obvious context clues in order to fill up more pages and generate "drama" by insisting on their own emotionalism.'

'Oh,' he said, a little surprised. 'Yes, you're right, that is what I was doing.'

'What it says here is his address. Rip is a mountain region in Czechia. It is just over an hour's drive. It is not very populated. But that appears to be his address, if we can find it ...'

'That's great,' he said. 'Let's go at once!'

'Mr Wangley?' said a voice. 'I'm afraid you will not be going anywhere ...'

40

Wangley looked up in astonishment. 'My god!' he said.

He gasped.

The group at the next table had suddenly transformed. One moment they appeared to be drably dressed balding men leaning in for a chat. An instant later, disguises cast off, they were revealed as a group of heavily muscled Japanese warriors wielding samurai swords, knuckledusters and ninja throwing stars that gleamed murderously under the pub lights.

'He will be coming with us,' said the leader of this group, coolly. 'The secret, and where it is hidden, belong to the Yakuza ...'

'Pardon me, señor!' said a voice from the next table. Another group of apparently elderly Irish men and women had shed their brown overcoats and stood armed with machetes, knives, guns and (the rumbling hum of an engine suddenly showed) a chainsaw. Cartel tattoos abounded on every visible inch of skin.

'He will be coming with us,' said the leader of this group in an accent that was certainly South American but harder to be more precise about. 'My employer wants answers, and he gets what he wants …'

'I think you'll find that Professor Wangley wants to come with us …' said another voice – an actually Irish one this time.

At a third table, three figures stood and turned. All were wearing monk-like cloaks. From their attire, they appeared to be a priest, a rabbi and an imam.

Richard gasped.

'My god!' he said. 'It's those three I saw earlier in that pub, what was it called? Declan O'Donnelly's, that's it. They must be on quite a bar crawl!'

'Don't be ridiculous, Richard,' said Marika, 'they've obviously been looking for the Secretest of Secretisms too. They got wind it was hidden in an Irish pub …'

She pointed. Each of them was cradling an Uzi in their arms. In their eyes were expressions not of spiritual understanding, but cold, hard reality. Determination and grit were etched in every bulging muscle and taut sinew visible beneath their ritual habiliments. They were here to get what they wanted and weren't prepared to leave without it. And so on and so forth.

Then the lights went out.

'*Pozhalysta*, all please be putting your guns down,' said a voice.

From behind the bar six figures rose into sight. Blinding head torches shone from their foreheads, and the automatic rifles they had all been carrying earlier, when Marika and Richard had seen them at the morgue, were present and correct.

'Mr Professor Richard is being coming with us. He have explaining to do.'

At that moment, a tense silence stretched between the parties, who were all wielding weapons. Stretched like a dough that quickly became too thin for a pizza, or even a naan, then a chapati, or even a wrapper for a Russian dumpling, Colombian *empañadas* or Japanese *gyoza* …

Finally, the possibility for the silence to form even a single layer of filo in a Middle-Eastern *börek* was exceeded.

At which point the silence exploded into a thunderous crash – but from a bewilderingly unexpected direction.

Everyone turned to the door to see what the sound could possibly be.

The doorframe was in pieces and glass was showering everywhere. It was as if it was being dismantled by a tremendous and casual strength, in the same way a child knocks down its toys.

From within the room the effect was like the visitation of some terrific supernatural power of destruction, a biblical storm or earthquake.

Framed in the doorway was a gigantic figure, almost impossibly tall and vast, more mountain than person. Having ripped through the frontage with seeming effortlessness, it seemed poised to come straight in and do the same to the people watching it.

There was another enormous silence filled with danger, fear and mortal dread. (And one or two sounds from the trouser regions of assembled clientele.)

Then the shooting started.

41

Richard grabbed Marika and threw both of them to the ground. Shards of glass and splinters of wood sprayed down around them as they wriggled along the floor. Bodies fell, and there were cries of pain and curses in a multitude of different languages ...

'Through here,' said Richard. He had found a hatch that led down to the cellar. The way was lit by the muzzle flashes of the firing guns all around them as they clambered into darkness, and let the lid shut above their heads.

They knocked against barrels and their feet slipped frustratingly on the wet floor, until they found a ladder that led up to the loading bay and the street outside. Moments later, they were in the alleyway behind the pub, and running as fast as they could, letting the shadows cloak them ...

'Thank god for these endless passageways,' said Marika.

Right now, the fact that this part of the historical Old Town had been built up over centuries, with no coherent street plan, was their friend.

Perhaps the only friend they had.

I'm not saying they didn't have fond acquaintances and loved ones in their daily lives, not a bit of it. I'm sure they did. But those people were not here right now, and were unable to help. And so the randomised road network was the only thing lending them assistance. In that way (and no other) it was their friend. No doubt if they came across this particular piece of urban geography again at a later date, the friendship may have cooled, perhaps for some reason even become antagonistic. Who knows. But right now ... hopefully, you get my point.

They turned first left then right, instinctively forming a random pattern of escape. Putting as many footsteps between themselves and the life-threatening violence behind them.

Turning down yet another narrow passage, they saw at the end it led onto a main street.

'Turn back?' Marika asked.

'No, keep going,' said the well-peer-reviewed professor. 'It'll take two seconds to rush across the road, and with luck we'll find our way into alleys on the other side, and be lost again.'

She looked unsure, and stopped.

'Trust me,' he said. He held his hand out.

She looked into his eyes. How much did she know this man? They had met just hours ago, and he had plunged her into the heart of a murderous conspiracy. Each of them had lost everything, they had gone on the run together and were facing peril in every direction. Somehow he seemed to attract danger and intrigue to himself, even though he was, all things considered, a rather banal individual.

And yet she looked into his eyes and thought she saw something there. Something worth trusting. Goodness, perhaps, or sincerity. Or the pained expression of someone whose backside is exposed to the midnight chill of the brisk

Czech winds. He had solved several arcane mysteries, and saved them from certain death. More than once.

If she was going to take a risk, she thought, *she might as well take it with him. Compared with other men she had known* ...

'Christ, make up your mind!' said Wangley. 'Stop just standing there!'

'Yes, I was just going to say yes!' she enthused.

She gave him her hand.

And they started running.

Just as they reached the end of the alley, a shape blocked it off. A black sedan came to a sharp stop, its brakes squeaking, the body of the car rocking on its wheels.

The rear door popped open. Inside was a man with a gun.

'Shit,' said Wangley.

42

Inside the car was a neat-looking man in his fifties, wearing a neatly cut navy-coloured hand-stitched suit and a neat pair of designer glasses. The handgun was clearly visible in a shoulder holster.

'Please, get in, Professor Wangley,' he said in a smooth-toned American accent. He adjusted his gold tie-pin, neatening it. 'Ms Novak.'

'Who are you?' Richard asked. Marika clutched his arm in fear. 'And why should I?'

'I'd like to get you away from here as fast as possible, and I'm a long way outside my jurisdiction,' said the man. 'My name is Caldwell Starkley. I'm afraid you are in serious danger …'

Richard looked in through the door and saw two serious-looking individuals in the front seats, each wearing suits.

'I assure you I work for the American people, professor,' said the man. 'I mean you no harm. Now please, we don't have much time …'

Richard and Marika looked at each other. Then they heard it. Behind them, footsteps were fast approaching.

Marika got in first and clipped herself in.

'Actually it would make more sense if you went in the middle,' Richard said. 'And I went on the passenger side. You're smaller than me and it would mean you get in the driver's eyeline less than I do.'

'Just get in, Richard!' she said.

'Yeah, okay. I mean, I don't mind going in the middle,' he said.

(He did mind. It made him feel like a child.)

The car zoomed away into the night and Wangley was thrust back into his seat. Soon they were away from the ancient narrow avenues of the Old Town, crossing a bridge and, seconds later, travelling at speed down broad boulevards dotted with trees and elegant cast-iron street lamps.

With profound gratitude, Wangley and Marika saw that the city was completely empty. Aside from an occasional car or lone pedestrian, there was no activity anywhere, no police blocks to impede their progress.

'We've been watching the events this evening with a great deal of consternation,' said Starkley sternly. He exuded natural authority and unruffled calm.

'It's been quite a night,' said Marika. 'Are you ... from the American embassy?'

'It's not important exactly who we are,' said Starkley darkly, 'only that we have insight into the goings on in the city and know when it's in our interests to protect an American citizen. First things first, professor. We have a change of clothes for you.'

He reached down by his feet, came up with a bag and dropped it in Richard's lap. Inside were jeans, a sweater and a T-shirt.

'Thank god,' said Richard. 'And thanks also for appearing just at that minute. It was a tight spot.'

'It's nothing. Literally. Officially, we never met. But with all these crimes happening in and around Prague, we wanted to prevent an international incident. Now, is there a place where we can take you, Ms Novak?'

'She's coming with me,' said Wangley firmly.

The two figures in the front exchanged a meaningful look.

'No can do, professor. We can offer you protection but not her. I was going to suggest that you bed down in the embassy and we put you on a flight back to the US in the morning.'

'But that's impossible!' said Wangley angrily. 'We're close to solving the mystery of what's happened. Susannah is missing! I may only have hours or even minutes to save her ...'

'There are a lot of moving parts in this situation, professor,' interrupted the navy-suited individual, 'and we don't know which parts are connected to each other. It's a volatile scenario, and developing at speed. International crime is involved ...'

'We narrowly escaped them only minutes ago,' said Marika.

'You were lucky,' said Starkley starchily. 'The Colombian cartel and the Yakuza, among other players ...'

'Why would they commit a series of murders in Prague?' wondered Richard. 'What are they after?'

'Have you heard of an outfit called the Elders of Athens?' Starkley asked sharply. They shook their heads. 'They are a semi-mythical group, who go back thousands of years. They are committed to the prevention of the use of the Philosopher's Stone. They think that it will mean the release of a superhuman evil that will bring about the end of the world. What the ancients referred to variously as Armageddon, or the opening of Pandora's Box.'

'Who are they, exactly?' asked Marika.

'We don't know. Nobody knows. But legend has it that once, sages from all different religions came together to ensure that alchemy, the process explained by Hermes Trismegistus in the Emerald Tablet and the *Secret of Secrets*, would never be achieved, and the Philosopher's Stone would remain unused. They decided to use whatever force necessary to prevent it. They have connections in every major city in the world.

'For two millennia or more, they have succeeded. But two decades ago, some dangerous piece of information came onto the market. We think it was uncovered here in Prague, when the flooding caused old alchemists' laboratories to be discovered, with elixirs and spells intact.

'By then, their organisation had changed. Although they represent all known religions, they had pretended to convert to Christianity. They kept to their strict rules – an all-male membership who practised fanatical fitness. And they set up clubs in plain sight, where no one would expect them to lurk. Here, they watched and they waited. And whenever two come across each other they repeat their mantra, which translates to: You must crush alchemy.'

'My god!' breathed Wangley wonderingly. 'The YMCA!'

'That explains the priest, rabbi and imam who tried to attack us just now,' said Marika.

'I'm afraid it does,' said Starkley sturdily. 'As for the other parties, what are they ever after? Money. Always money.'

'But somehow they're mixed up in something that's steeped in alchemy, magic, supernatural forces,' said Richard, 'and pacts with the devil.'

He explained what he knew about Lukas Prochezka.

'I'm impressed,' said Starkley heartily. 'Despite being on the run, you've managed to find out a lot.'

'We've also got information that you haven't,' said Marika. 'A clue, written in an ancient code, left by one of the murder victims.'

Richard fished in his cleavage and brought it out. The other man looked at it with deep interest.

'It led us to an Irish pub where the victim was apparently a regular patron. Left there was another message.' Richard produced the second piece of evidence.

Marika explained their near encounter with the Russian armed forces in the morgue. The evidence which had been taken.

'The second code is the one we now need to crack,' said Richard, struggling out of his costume and trying to avoid elbowing either of the others in the face. 'Can you help me get my arm ... thank you ... That's better ...'

'Have you got any information that can help us?' Marika asked. 'We're wanted for murder. As well as the destruction of several famous and highly valuable works of art.'

'Damn these criminals,' said Starkley staunchly. 'Don't they have any morals?'

'Exactly!' said Wangley. 'Terrible, *terrible* people.'

Marika gave him a curious look from the corner of her eye, as he finished putting on the jeans.

'Any help you can give ... Any intelligence you may have received ...' Marika pressed.

'Ma'am, I cannot stress enough that we are not involved in this case in any way. In fact, we are agents from the Federal Food and Drug Administration.'

Marika was taken aback.

'I guess ... when I saw the gun, I thought ...'

'We have to deal with some pretty tough grocers,' said Starkley calmly.

'Right ...' said Wangley warily. 'But I've been thinking. There is someone who might be able to help. An old colleague who lives off the grid, with no phone, in the middle of nowhere. He is living at Rip, a mountain thirty miles north of Prague.'

Starkley gave a few brisk words of commandment to his colleagues in the front seat. At once the car slowed, went into a turn, then accelerated off in a new direction.

'We'll drop you there,' he said.

43

In under an hour, the black sedan was creeping slowly along a mountain path. It came to a halt and the door opened.

Out from it stepped first Marika, and then a very different looking Professor Wangley. He turned to offer thanks to their saviours, but the car moved off at once, and at speed, drawing the door shut as it sped away.

Richard looked after it, the pained expression in his eyes barely visible in the moonlight.

'What is it, Richard?' she asked him. She thought for a moment. 'Oh! You wanted to ask to keep the costume?'

Wangley looked startled. 'No! No, no, of course not,' he chuckled uncertainly. Then he glanced at the retreating car again as it vanished out of sight, and sighed.

'I'm sure they're available on the internet,' she offered.

'We must be close,' the professor said, looking at the terrain. 'This is his exact address. But I can't see anything ...'

'Me neither,' admitted the young European woman. 'Do you know what you're looking for?'

'Something pretty basic, I guess,' said Wangley. 'He always said he planned to get away from the rat race, go and live a simple mountain existence. Pure air, spring water, chopping his own chickens, raising wood, that sort of thing. Ah, it will be so good to see him again,' Richard said. 'So intelligent, so kind. Always laughing. He loved to laugh!'

'Everyone loves to laugh, Richard,' said Marika, as they struggled through some waist-high undergrowth. 'That's like saying he liked food.'

'You've got him in a nutshell. He loved food! Food and laughing. But never laughing *at* food. That was a big thing with him. Made him really angry. I wonder why. Anyway – what a man. I'm guessing we'd be looking for a rustic cabin …'

'Like that one?'

Luckily it was a clear night with a bright, waxing moon. Although the cabin was deliberately set back from the track so as to be inconspicuous, they soon made out its straight lines against the trees, and saw yellow light leaking out around the curtains.

'He's up,' said Richard. 'Always was a night owl …'

Together, they walked up the wooden stairs to the veranda. Tentatively, Richard reached out and knocked on the wooden door.

There was a sound of sudden movement within, and then the light around the curtains went out.

'I'm really sorry to come at this time of night, Jaroslav,' said Richard in a loud voice. 'But I need your help. It's me! Richard Wangley!'

'There is nobody here,' said a growling voice. 'Go away.'

'Please, I have no one else to turn to. You're my last hope!'

'You're not listening. There is no one here! Leave me alone!' said the voice, even more angrily.

'Is that his voice?' Marika whispered in Richard's ear.

He nodded. It was – but he sounded different.

Aged. *Decades* older.

Richard wondered what could possibly have caused this to happen to his beloved mentor since their last meeting in the early 1990s.

'You are Professor Jaroslav Sedlak, born 1946 in Kraków, to Czech parents,' Richard said. 'I'm your former pupil!'

'I know nobody called Vangly,' said the voice. 'How do I know it is even you?'

'You taught me when I spent a year at Budapest in 1991,' said Wangley. 'We met again at a conference in Oslo in 1993, and had martinis at the bar. Things sure got messy that night, huh? You remember me now, right?'

'Oh, it's *that* asshole,' the voice said quietly, to itself. There was a squeak of springs, as of someone getting off a mattress. 'What the hell do you mean by coming and waking an old man up? Who sent you? Maybe you are here to spy on me!'

'I've been framed for murder and am on the run with this attractive young woman from mysterious forces, with seemingly magical powers. We are hoping to solve a mystery that might lead to unbelievably gigantic amounts of money ...'

Within the cabin, there was a pause.

'Okay,' said the voice, slightly less sleepy than before. 'Now I have to admit I am reluctantly interested ...'

There was the click of a latch being pulled back.

44

Then there was the snap of a padlock being opened. And the rattle of a chain being removed. Four more heavy metallic noises followed as deadbolts were pulled back.

Followed by three more keys turning in heavy locks.

At last the door opened, just an inch.

'Put these facemasks on,' said Sedlak, handing them out.

The door widened to admit them. When they came inside, and it was shut behind them, they found themselves in a bleak, empty cabin.

'But Jaroslav!' said Richard. 'What happened to your library! I thought you were going to live in the mountains and compose your great Encyclopaedia of Secretical Symbologism?'

'Why bother?' said the man before them. He was scrawny and in dirty, threadbare pyjamas. 'The government would never let it come out anyway. They control everything. I only realised how naïve I'd always been during the lockdown, when I discovered that they were listening to everything we do. Trying to make us take their vaccines!'

He was getting emotional, hopping from one foot to another. Richard decided to calm things down.

'Do you think I could get a cup of water, Jaroslav?' he asked. 'I'm very thirsty after being chased by armed thugs all evening ...'

'Of course,' said the older man. 'Where are my manners? One for you too?' Marika assented, and he went into the backroom. He was gone some time and when he came back he placed two cups on the table, then stood back. He was now wearing a full hazmat suit, his face visible through a plastic visor.

They sipped their water, while Sedlak stood stiffly by and watched them.

Richard outlined their adventures so far this evening. Sedlak grew more engrossed as the tale went on, even gasping and laughing at certain moments. Finally, Richard placed the piece of paper with the second code in front of him. He sat down, taking a pencil, which had to be placed into the clumsy glove of his suit by Marika, and made a few scattered notes on the back of an old scrag of newspaper.

'It's straightforward enough,' Sedlak said thoughtfully. 'It's like the previous code. The script is ancient Assyrian – and the language is demotic Egyptian. Not hieroglyphs, which was the priestly language, but the language of the people.'

'What does it say?' Richard asked, leaning forward. Marika did too.

Jaroslav turned the paper round. They all read it. Then read it again.

'What does it mean?' Richard asked.

'Hopefully something,' Sedlak replied. 'Mean anything to you, young lady?'

On the scrap of newspaper was written:

CRSE136JP

Marika shook her head sadly. 'Could be the codename of a file in some kind of filing system,' she said.

'Could almost be a car numberplate – but not from any country I know of,' said Richard.

'It must mean something. The answer's in what you've already learned this evening ...' said Sedlak. 'You finished with those?'

Both the water glasses stood empty. They nodded.

Sedlak produced a pair of tongs and one by one picked up the tumblers, took them over to his fireplace, which was burning fiercely, and dropped them in.

'No offence,' he said, when he saw their looks. 'You might still be government agents trying to impregnate my bloodstream with your chemicals.'

'The key to the mystery,' said Richard, keen to change the subject, 'is Lukas Prochezka. I'm convinced once we find out whatever happened to him, where he's been all this time, all will become clear.'

'Oh, that guy!' said Jaroslav, smiling – although only half his face was visible through the visor of his suit. 'Yeah. Lukas lives next door.'

Marika and Richard gave him a sad look. The man did indeed seem quite deranged. What a desperate existence he had here, on this lonely mountain. No wonder his brain had wandered ...

'I mean it,' he said. 'Just a hundred yards along. Next cabin. These woods are filled with people who've tried to get away from society. There's him, Satoshi Nakamoto, Thomas Pynchon ... We have a bridge evening, last Thursday of the month.'

Richard went to a window and peeked out in the direction Sedlak had indicated. Outside, all was darkness.

'Just along there, you say?' he asked. '*He's still alive?*'

'Sure. Go and knock. He stays up late like me. Tell him he can have some of my schnitzelberry jello. Just made today. My grandmother's recipe. And tell that *putz* I want my badminton racquet back!'

45

'He must be mistaken,' said Marika, as they walked along the mountain path.

'He certainly didn't seem to be his old self,' said Richard. 'His mind has wandered...'

'Maybe he was just trying to get rid of us,' Marika said. 'But if he's right, what can it mean?'

'We're getting close to the solution to the mystery,' said Richard. 'I can feel it. Just the answer to a few more questions and everything will fall into place. One more piece of information, and the key will be unlocked...'

'A metaphor, Richard!' Marika said. 'Now I understand!'

Richard was pleased. Then he saw that Marika was holding up a flower to him that she had picked.

'Yes, nice,' he said.

'Mmm, metaphors! I like the way they smell!' she said, holding it to her nose. She started to skip, pleased with herself.

As they followed the path they had been instructed to take, they found their way obscured by trees. But as they got closer, the apparent barrier proved to be illusory, and branches parted easily to admit them.

In the moonlight they could see a building up ahead – a quaint, tottering woodman's cottage, with a brick chimney from which spilled a gentle stream of smoke.

'Stop right there,' said a voice, when they were still ten feet short of the door.

Bright lights flashed on, making them blink. They felt trapped. Richard put his hands up.

'I've got weapons trained on you. Go back where you came from! This is your last warning ...'

'Suspicious lot on this mountain,' Marika said quietly.

'I don't know who you think I am,' called Richard. 'But I'm just an American professor ... I'm truly sorry for the late hour ... I know how this must look ...'

'Looks damn suspicious,' said the voice. Richard saw it was coming from a little speaker above the door. 'Why don't you just go away, and we can forget about this?'

'I can't,' said Richard.

The speaker remained inactive. Insects and animals scurried to get into or out of the glaring and incongruous light.

'If I'm speaking to Lukas Prochezka,' said Richard, 'I'm afraid I've got grave news about your son, Jakub ...'

With a snap, the lights went out.

Richard half expected the next moment he was going to be pumped full of holes from some concealed weapon.

Then the latch clacked, and the door swung open.

46

'Nothing could give me greater sadness,' said Richard, 'than to pass on such news.'

He was sitting on a chair by a rustic wooden table. Marika was sitting next to him, keeping silent, while their host took in what was being relayed to him.

The man before them was nearly fifty. He was greying, but slender and fit looking. Dressed in humble, much-patched clothes, a weary, wary intelligence gleamed from his wearily intelligent (but wary) eyes.

The interior of the cottage was stocked with essentials on every shelf, bottles of pickled vegetables, dented pans, bushels of herbs and piles of kindling. A fire in the grate sent weak light into the room, lending it a sombre air.

'I knew something like this would happen,' Prochezka said quietly. 'I've known for some time ...'

'I'm so sorry,' said Marika.

'Lots of things have happened. We are on the run, framed for your son's murder. I think the killers wanted us – the police, everyone – to think he was you. Naturally the DNA they had on file for you was over two decades old, from when the technology was simpler. It makes sense that you and he would have near-identical test results. But they wanted to trick us,' Richard went on. 'To make us think that something supernatural was going on. That magic was happening in this town, alchemy ...'

'Alchemy!' Prochezka said, confused. 'Alchemy *is* happening in this town. Did you not know it?'

Marika and Richard looked at each other. This was not the reaction they expected. Perhaps in his grief, the man was searching for a distraction.

'What do you mean?' Richard asked gently.

'Alchemy is – in its most basic sense – turning base metals into gold. Lead, for instance.'

'Right,' agreed Marika.

'They are doing that now. Right now. Two years ago, Prague University acquired the world's most powerful particle accelerator. With it, you can literally alter the make-up of atoms – as yet, only one atom at a time. But think about it. Alchemy literally *is* possible. And it's being done in Prague, the city of alchemy ...' Speaking quietly, he drifted to a halt.

'They're all dead,' said Richard. 'The Experimental Physics Unit. Murdered.'

Lukas stared at him in wonder at this news. 'They messed with forces they did not understand,' he said under his breath.

'Didn't Jakub do that too?' Richard asked. 'He was meddling with something. Was it alchemy?'

'No,' said Prochezka quietly. 'Jakub had no interest in physics. I don't know what he was working on. We hadn't spoken for many years ...' He became abstracted again and looked down at his hands.

Richard stood up, went to a shelf and took down a glass bottle and three tumblers. He poured all three of them a measure and handed one to Prochezka, who took it with a grateful nod and downed it. Then he handed the glass back.

'That's water by the way. The *Becherovka* is in that brown jug, over the fireplace.'

'Can I tell you what I think happened?' Richard asked, as he refilled the glass with herbal liqueur. Prochezka nodded, not meeting his eyes.

'You were working in Prague's Silicon Basement. Making all these businesses that were worth millions, if not billions.'

'Many billions,' said Prochezka.

'You found something. Something ancient. Maybe it was an alchemist's elixir. Maybe it was an algebraic equation or an incantation. But you realised you had stumbled on the Philosopher's Stone. You were tempted. You were riding high. The dot-com bubble had already burst, and you were doing okay. Then, soon after, were the floods of 2002, the whole city under water. Something changed.'

Prochezka refilled his glass.

'Something scared you. More than just the flood. So you took what money you could, and moved out here. People thought you were dead – that's what you wanted them to think. You had a partner, or perhaps met one locally. And had a baby. Lived off grid. Raised your son away from the technology that had brought you fame – and horror. How am I doing so far?'

Prochezka had been frowning in concentration. He nodded. 'Not exactly correct, but ... not entirely *in*correct ...' he said.

Marika, who by this point had developed a thorough hatred of exposition, had found a Rubik's Cube and was playing with it, while half listening.

'You could not bring yourself to destroy all your computers. They were too much part of you, and you part of them,' said Richard. 'Jakub found them. And here, away from society, on this mountain, it was too cruel to deprive him of that. He took to them naturally, like you. He started to build them. And once he got as good as you had been, you were afraid. He was becoming what you had been. You tried to take them away. And it caused a rift.'

'I'll save you time,' said Prochezka exhaustedly. 'He found the structure of an AI model I had been developing. It was brilliant. He took it further – much further. And you know what he called it? Mephistopheles! As though subconsciously he knew the danger he was facing! He programmed it to solve the world's problems. Inequality. Disease. Climate change. I begged him not to switch it on ...'

'The Philosopher's Stone,' said Richard quietly. 'You found it ... but *you* didn't use it!'

Prochezka looked up in surprise. 'How did you know?' he asked.

'It doesn't make sense, that someone who already has the world at his fingertips would make a deal with the devil – and then vanish to live quietly in a cottage. If you sell your soul, you are supposed to get twenty-four years of success and fame before the debt gets called in. And no offence, this place is hardly a three-floor penthouse in Vegas.'

Prochezka seemed to relax, as his secret came out.

'You could have opened this Pandora's Box, you could have been Prometheus, giving the secret of fire to mere mortals.

Turning them from golems into people. But you chose to keep it secret.'

'This isn't right,' said Marika, looking up. 'He's got it. We know he has.'

Prochezka shook his head. 'I didn't want it. I couldn't handle that danger. I didn't have such an ego. But my poor boy, who grew up away from society, he didn't understand the dangers like I did.'

'I think he *did* use the Philosopher's Stone, maybe just glancingly, thought he'd try it just once. But then it was already too late. He built this software of his, this Mephistopheles, using the Philosopher's Stone. But it was too powerful …'

'The things we create destroy us,' said Prochezka with his eyes closed. 'Even though we love them.'

'What happened then, Marika?' Richard asked.

The Rubik's Cube clattered to the floor — unfinished.

She stared at him. Then turned to look at Lukas.

'Only you can finish the story,' said Richard. 'The computer did things he never expected. And you were there to watch, am I right?'

The light was dim in the cottage, but Richard distinctly saw the look on her face turn hard and determined for a moment. Before switching in an instant to one of puzzled, vulnerable femininity.

'What do you mean, Richard? We met by chance tonight …'

'I didn't believe that for a second. Well,' he confessed, 'a man has pride. A few seconds, perhaps.'

She shook her head and laughed. A clear, beautiful sound. 'What is this!' she said. Richard thought he had never seen a woman look more convincingly innocent. *What a talent*, he thought. *Just a shame that talent had been used for deceit, betrayal – and lots of murder.*

'Your performance was good,' he said, 'but not perfect. You slipped a few times. When you saw it was Jakub's body you couldn't believe your eyes. You said, "Why would they do this?" And a few moments later, you said to me that you were in trouble. I assumed it was the camaraderie of the moment. We were being shot at after all. Perhaps you thought that I'd forget.'

'He's been through a lot ...' Marika said to their host. 'He's getting paranoid.'

'You're the woman he told me about,' said Lukas. 'He said he'd found someone who had the same ideals as he. I was so glad for him. I wanted to meet you. Meet you both.'

'When he switched Mephistopheles on,' said Richard, 'it went haywire. Maybe he asked it how to save the world. And it replied: kill all humans, then the world will be saved. Maybe he *ordered* it to save the world. And in the few hours or days that it was active, all hell broke loose.'

Marika didn't jump in, so Richard continued.

'It took money from the worst people in the world in order to do good – perhaps deceiving them by offering huge returns ... setting up a crypto exchange or something like that. That's where all the criminals hang out nowadays. Next thing, they were on your trail ...'

'We could have saved the world,' said Marika, her voice low and mean. 'And we could have made a lot of money at the same time. It was at our fingertips. But he refused to take *anything*. From saving the world! Leaving us open, unprotected. It was mad.'

'And once the AI was switched off, the money was gone,

redistributed, couldn't be found again?' Richard suggested. 'And the bad people it was stolen from came knocking. What they want, if they can be negotiated with, is to reclaim the Philosopher's Stone. And turn it to their own ends. And Jakub refused, even under torture.'

'But he knew *you* could find it and destroy it,' Marika said. 'And so did I.'

'So although he'd used it, he didn't have it any more,' Richard said. He nodded. Now he understood. 'That makes sense. He knew he was going to be killed. I'm guessing it was those Russian special forces, who have a penchant for throwing people out of windows. They told you to be by the Astronomical Clock. Demanding that you find the Stone and bring it to them. And you collected me ...'

'I knew Jakub loved codes,' said Marika. 'I knew he would send a message in code, if he could. And you were the person who would be most likely to be able to break it. After your previous adventures.'

'So you kidnapped my girlfriend,' Richard said. 'You thought that would work?'

'I know nothing about that,' said Marika. Richard was bewildered. He shook his head to try and clear it, and pursued his line of logic.

'You thought they were going to meet you in person, give you an ultimatum, some way out, to save his life. But instead they dumped his body from above. That's why I could hear thumping in my ears – it was the blades of a chopper. And they framed us both.'

'Enough talking,' said Marika. 'They'll be here in minutes. They've been following us all along. Tell us where it is, or we're all dead. All three of us.'

Richard produced the code. Put it on the table. Prochezka came forward and looked at it.

CRSE136JP

He shook his head sadly.

'I have no idea what this is,' he said. 'And if I'm going to die tonight, I'm ready.'

'You *must* know!' Marika shrieked. She picked the paper up and thrust it in his face. In her desperation, Richard realised this was her last ploy. She had promised the bounty to her enemies. 'You *saw* it!' she said. 'It was you who Jakub stole it from!'

There was a vibration in the room, which was turning to a thrumming noise.

'I wish I'd never found it,' Prochezka said, sadly. 'There we were in those caves under the street. Then one day a wall collapsed and there was a lot of rotten stuff, and this book in the middle of it. With a name on the front: Cly something Ricardus.'

'Sir Clyffe Rycharde,' said Wangley. 'The famous English magician. He lived in Prague and spent his life looking for the Philosopher's Stone. That book must have belonged to him!'

'*Tell* me where it is!' yelled Marika. She'd grabbed a knife, and was walking towards Lukas. 'Where is it?'

'I burned it,' Prochezka said. 'I promise you. I give you my word ...'

'You've got it memorised!' shouted Marika. 'Or someone copied it! Tell me!'

Prochezka nodded. 'My colleague at the time, Pugliach. He's doing strange things at the university these days.

Unnatural experiments. I'm afraid he may have memorised it ... If so, he's on his way to hell.'

The thrumming became a thumping. The timbers of the cottage shook and pictures on the walls rattled in their frames. A helicopter was close, getting closer, possibly overhead ...

An expression of peace settled over Prochezka as he turned to look at her. 'I made sure it would be forgotten,' he said. 'I sent it home. I've been waiting for this day!'

And as he started to laugh, lights flashed in through the windows ...

47

Alphonso was lost. A new feeling had spread through him. Something desperate and overpowering.

He had loved, and lost. And it had ruined everything.

When he had met his new female friend at the pottery class, they had spoken afterwards to each other. Haltingly, with great embarrassment.

But they had agreed to meet the following day.

And so they had sat and eaten a picnic, looking out over the Vltava River. They smiled a lot. And looked a trifle goofy.

I am happy, he'd thought. *I am happy now. I am alive and happy.*

She had seemed happy. He had felt happy that she had seemed happy.

He was starting to think about asking if they could meet again.

And then something had happened. A little buzzing noise. She looked at a small machine in her hand, and her body had gone rigid. She had stood, and walked away.

Alphonso watched her robotic movements. Too stunned to do anything until she moved out of sight. Then he got to his feet and followed.

He had seen her go to a place in the city. He had hidden and watched from the corner of the street, as she had broken the door down. Screams came from within. And his friend had emerged, covered with blood, and staring dully ahead.

He followed her to her home. Saw her go in.

And then went to his own place. And lay in the darkness, and thought.

The following day, he had met with a friend from the old country. A fellow who seemed to think it was his duty to look after Alphonso. Although he had been feeling increasingly this was no longer necessary. He was by now wily enough to put on his old clothes before meeting this person, so as not to create suspicion.

'It's over, Alphonso Emmettio,' said his friend. 'The job is finished. It's time to go home. Your work is done.'

'Me not want to go home,' Alphonso said.

'Here's your ticket. And your passport. I've written the time of the plane here. I'll be at the airport. Hey, you still got your name written on your forehead, where I wrote it so you could see it. Let me rub it off for you ...'

'Me not go home,' said Alphonso.

'We done a good job, my boy. We protected the interests of our Sicilian grocers. We smashed some competition. They're happy with us, back home. Okay?' And finishing his drink, the man was gone into the crowd.

Alphonso had not gone to the plane. He had gone to meet up with his female acquaintance, who was called Zalinka. He had reached the Irish pub where they had agreed to go on a date. But as she reached the door to go in, there had been another buzz on the electrical item in her pocket and she had turned robotically, to perform another of her mystical tasks.

Alphonso's heart quivered, vibrated — in fury he destroyed the doorway of the pub before he knew what he was doing.

He had been watching carefully as she carried out tasks for her master over the past week. He knew there was no communicating with her until the job was done. So he trailed behind.

She had walked slowly out to the university, and he was just a few steps behind.

When they had finished, and the flames were roaring into the sky, the whole of the Experimental Physics Department and everything in it was destroyed.

And he saw that she was signalling for rescue. To whom, he couldn't imagine.

She put her arms out wide above her head: Y. Then folded the forearms in towards her head: M. Bent her torso over to the left with her arms outstretched: C. And met her arms over her head, pointing upwards: A.

A light flashed in the distance. The call was answered. Rescue was coming ...

48

Burrrrr ... burrrr ... burrrrrrrrr ...

Wangley had heard nothing more of the conversation. He knew now that the Philosopher's Stone, whatever it was, whether a chemical equation or a poem or a sequence of numbers, would not be exposed tonight.

At first he saw in Lukas's eyes a confidence that he had long ago forgotten the secret of the Philosopher's Stone, either through failing memory, sheer determination or some more direct agency like hypnosis. The man was not afraid of revealing the secret.

And then – with a long, anxious glance to Richard – he communicated something crucial.

Richard knew at once that the man had long prepared a way of ensuring all knowledge of the Philosopher's Stone was eradicated from his brain forever.

Marika was shouting and threatening. Not paying close attention. At first Richard thought Lukas was blinking back tears. Or starting to have some kind of fit. Then the man met and held eyes with him, and started blinking again.

Richard saw the blinks were in a set pattern.

Morse code. Thank god for the Boy Scouts, he thought to himself, as he began to translate.

The message was simple. When he understood it, Richard felt his blood freeze.

Run. Now.

Marika was losing control, starting to hit Lukas, as Richard crept to the back of the cottage, unlatched a back door and spied a path to the cover of the trees.

Then, just at the moment when the noise of the incoming forces grew deafening, he'd sprinted ...

Burrrrr ... burrrr ... burrrrrrrrr ...

'Pick up!' he said. 'Dang it!'

He moved from foot to foot, and looked at the full moon, whose impervious and beneficent face had sunk close to the horizon.

As he had leapt over the fence at the back of the property and then raced through the mountain woods, catching his feet on roots and brambles, Richard thought from the sound of it that the helicopter must now be directly above the cottage.

He had found himself praying to the god he believed in – the god of Newton and Einstein – that he was far enough away when—

The explosion seemed to pick him up and spin the world beneath him. He catapulted through some bushes, rolled, then got up groggily. Felt some aches, but nothing broken. Behind him there was a terrible, violent concussion, followed by a second, deeper explosion that lit the woods around him for a quarter of a mile with a mottled orange light.

Must be the explosive Prochezka had deliberately set off, annihilating his own cottage, and the subsequent crash of the overhead helicopter, Wangley concluded.

He tried not to think about the loss of life happening so nearby. And, shakily at first, ran.

Burrrrrr ... Burrrrrrrrrr ...

Now, two hours later, after stumbling over wild terrain and then along country roads, here he was at a rusty old public phone on the wall of a closed petrol station. He couldn't believe it when, lifting the handset, he had found a dial tone.

Click.

'Hello?' said an uncertain voice, very distant.

'My god!' he said. 'Thank goodness you answered. Is that the office of Tristram Friegler?'

'It is,' said the voice.

'This is Tristram's author, Richard Wangley!' he said. 'Boy, am I glad to get through to you! Listen, my life is in danger. Once before, Tristram sent the publisher's helicopter to pick me up. I need it again. Can you send it?'

'Professor Wangley,' replied Madison, Tristram's assistant. 'Tristram has inherited wealth. That vehicle was not owned by Farrar, Straus and Giroux. I'm sure I can arrange a train ticket for you, third class? Payable against your advance, of course? If you give me your current address, I would be happy to raise a request internally and it should be with you in fifteen working days after approval. Would you like to proceed? Or can I help you with anything else?'

Richard let out an animal noise of dismay. 'Can you put Tristram on?'

'He's not with us any more,' said Madison. 'He's currently working in the Trump administration.'

Wangley dropped the handset back onto the receiver as though his fingers had been pricked by an electric shock.

He looked around him. On the other side of the street there was a dog licking something small and dead in the gutter.

The phone rang, making him jump.

'There will be a vehicle for you shortly,' said a voice. Then the line went dead.

As he walked out to the road he became aware of the hum of a car's engine. There it was, idling twenty yards away in the shadow of a derelict church.

'That was quick,' he said to himself. He walked over to it. Knocked on the window. The back door opened and he climbed in.

He sat in a fold-down seat facing backwards. Opposite him was an exceptionally neat-looking and sharply attractive woman with a briefcase on her lap. She wasted no time.

'Ethan Hunt,' she said coolly. 'Considering your reputation, I was surprised you were prepared to sell us the hard drive with all your agents' real identities on it. Hand it over and I will transfer the money to your account. Although I'd appreciate it if you'd take off that unconvincing rubber mask that looks like an ageing Tom Hanks ...'

'No, no,' Richard said. 'Wrong car, sorry. Sorry!' He stumbled out and slammed the door, then moved off as quickly as he could.

Further up the hill he saw a black sedan under a tree, with its parking lights on. He waited for the door to open, then climbed in.

A man in dark glasses and business suit regarded him carefully.

'Mr Bourne,' he said. 'You are a hard man to get hold of. I apologise for my agents being a tad ... overzealous. I trust you have the proof that it was the Senator who ordered the assassi—'

'No! That's not me! Nothing to do with me!' Richard said, jumping out.

'What is it with Prague and spies?' Wangley asked the night air, exasperated, when he was fifty yards away.

When he got a little further up the country road, a car sped into sight and then braked when it came level with him. The window wound down and he saw Caldwell Starkley.

'Well, if it isn't my favourite member of the Federal Food and Drug Administration …' said Wangley wearily.

49

'For a Harvard professor, you've got a pretty good record of surviving some damned complex and dangerous situations,' said Caldwell Starkley smarmily.

'Thank you,' said Wangley sanguinely, relaxing into the side seat this time, like an adult. 'It was a real close call that time, I admit. Tonight's been a long haul ...'

'So many irreplaceable artworks destroyed,' said Starkley harshly.

'Infuriating!' agreed Wangley worriedly but relievedly, as the car's acceleration caused him to sink relaxedly into its plush leather interior.

'You've been helpful in bringing several of the rogue elements at large in Prague tonight to heel,' said Starkley warmly. 'Many of the gang members who were injured or killed in the Heart O'Prague pub were wanted fugitives. We feel it's likely there will be the remains of many other bad actors discovered at the mountain cottage explosion site.'

'Prochezka was holed up there,' Richard said. 'When he realised he'd been located by his son's killers, he set off some kind of explosive he had secreted in his house. In fact, I now wonder if that was what was meant by the phrase "secretest of secretisms". The bomb that would ensure the dangerous information never came to light.'

The car sped on while he explained everything that had happened. By the end his head was spinning. There was more than he could take in.

'That explains a lot,' said Starkley smartly. 'The Golem murders were all leading towards the university ...'

'Kittling, Rabinowicz, Salz, Bialystock,' said Richard. 'This Pugliach person was using the Philosopher's Stone to perform some dangerous experiments ...'

'"Was" being the correct term,' said Starkley smugly. He said something to the driver and the car came to a halt. They got out and found themselves on a rise overlooking the city.

'My god,' said Richard. He couldn't take his eyes off it.

'A tragic sight,' admitted Starkley softly. 'But perhaps inevitable, considering the forces they were meddling with.'

Below them, several miles away, there was a giant conflagration. Dozens of fire trucks were arranged round a huge building covered in flames. It was a torch in the night sky.

'We don't know what happened,' said Starkley stolidly. 'Perhaps we'll never know. But I think it's over now. Which leaves one important thing – that second code you found.'

Richard pulled the piece of paper from his pocket and looked at it again.

CRSE136JP

'I think I know what it means,' Richard said. 'And I've got an idea I know where to go, to deal with it.'

Starkley looked impressed.

'But what kills me is Susannah!' Richard said, his stomach lurching. 'Where is she now? Please tell me she wasn't killed?'

'Hardly,' said Starkley archly, handing him a sheet of paper. 'She got away – and far from tardily.'

Richard had to get back into the car to read its contents. And then he understood – part of it, at least.

'Good luck, then,' said Starkley sleekly. 'We'll take you to a small airport where we've chartered a private plane. There's only one other passenger, but I'd stay away from him. An American citizen who's been on hold to easyJet for three days straight. He could blow at any time. Best if you both leave the city tonight, after everything that's happened.'

Wangley nodded.

'Good luck with your dangerous grocers,' said Richard.

'Oh, we feel confident that problem's been resolved tonight, too,' said Starkley balmily, as the car sped towards the plane home.

50

Esteemed expert in Secretismic Symboligisticism Richard Wangley frowned.

He was confused. Unsure of what was going on.

He turned the book he was reading round, and looked at the cover. It was a copy of *Room* by Emma Donoghue. He was reading it in response to a comment from his brother-in-law Hank that had stuck with him, as Hank's observations often seemed to.

'You know, Richard,' he had said, 'you really *don't know how to read the room*.'

Now Richard was halfway through the book, and he found it perfectly easy to read. Not the most cheerful piece of fiction he'd ever encountered, but far from difficult to comprehend. Once again, he found himself baffled by Hank.

He had been sat for a long time with his glass of warm ale, waiting for closing time, which was finally nearly here. He took the piece of paper out of his pocket, and looked at it again.

CRSE136JP

He was sure he was right.

It had taken some searching, but he was finally here.

In an incredibly succinct code, Jakub Prochezka had indicated the final resting place of the Philosopher's Stone.

The only magician who had ever claimed to have it in his possession had been the Elizabethan magician Sir Clyffe Rycharde. It made sense, then, that if there was one final copy in existence, he had brought it home with him when he had returned to England in 1603.

After landing at Dover he had come back to his family home, a manor house in the lonely marshy wastes many miles beyond the nearest town or village.

In the intervening centuries, however, many things had changed.

The family's fortunes had collapsed, and the house had fallen into ruin and been destroyed. Meantime the city of London had expanded south of the Thames and then swelled steadily for centuries, until it even swallowed up the location of the Rycharde abode, formerly a day's coach ride from the city gates.

The code, then, was: CR for Clyffe Rycharde, and the rest was a British postcode giving a precise address. An address that was today the location of a pub.

Wangley had come here the day before and spoken to several staff members. Money had changed hands. Promises had been made. And now, as the final customers were being ushered out of the Lewisham Wetherspoons and the doors were locked, a solemn gathering commenced.

The staff were turning a blind eye to what went on, and had 'accidentally' left keys to the cellar on the bar.

'It's definitely down there?' Richard asked.

Three robed figures joined him by the entrance to the cellar, which was a square in the floor. He looked at them: a priest, a rabbi and an imam. They all nodded. They lifted the latch in the floor and climbed down.

Between the beer barrels and the cooler was a rickety, nearly rotted wooden door. The priest held a torch as Wangley opened it. From here, a staircase led even further downwards, between mossy walls of stone.

At the bottom of the staircase was a chamber, carved out of white rock. It was chilly and eerily quiet, all the noise of London (and even that of the pub machinery) blocked out.

In the middle was a stone sarcophagus.

'You'd better be right this time, Richard,' said the rabbi.

The imam nodded. 'This had better be the true resting place we're destroying,' he said.

'Don't want a repeat of the Sycamore Gap mistake,' said the priest.

'Or that historical business with the Crooked House pub in Staffordshire,' said the rabbi. 'We barely got away with that. You're *sure* this time?'

'This time I'm right. It's here,' Richard said fervently. 'Look inside! You'll see!'

The rabbi and the imam lifted the stone lid, their muscles straining. It remained stubborn for a few seconds against their conjoined strength but then moved with a heavy grinding sound. The priest pointed the torch inwards.

And from the gloom within, Wangley pulled out a centuries-old grimoire, bound in leather. It was decorated all over with cabalistic symbols, and exuded a smell of herbs and dank paper.

They all gasped.

'Now we burn it ...' said the rabbi, bring out a metal bowl and a flask of lighter fluid.

Richard looked on, feeling equal parts sadness and wonder. Sadness at what was being lost, and wonder that he was here to see it.

The imam lit a match that flared brilliantly in the darkness for just a moment. They all watched as the flame steadied.

Then he let go.

51

'Are you here for the book signing?' asked the girl behind the till, excitedly.

'Oh, you betcha,' said Richard. He gave her a wolfish grin. He took his seat at the back of the poky little alternative bookstore, sipped his cold-foam chicory iced latte and waited for the author with a deep sense of anticipation.

It was good to be in New York. Back on American soil after his latest adventure. Which he was determined would be his last. From now on an adventure for him was a nice book to read and early to bed. That was undoubtedly some excellent advice he'd received from ...

'Ladies and gentlemen, I'm thrilled to announce Susannah Moses,' proclaimed the feeble voice of a bookseller unaccustomed to public speaking, from behind some shelves.

After some preparatory remarks, Susannah gave a short reading from her book. Richard had already read it, of course, but he enjoyed it more this time round. And in a different way.

He kept himself hidden at the back and did not contribute to the Q&A that followed. When Susannah had finished signing books, he made sure he was the final person to approach her table. She flashed her automatic and professional smile at him, before she saw who it was.

'Hullo, Susannah,' he said.

'Richard!' she said.

'When you went missing I didn't know what to believe,' he said. 'There was so much hearsay. Rumours,' he said.

'A lot of "He said she said"?' she said. 'He said you'd come here,' she said.

'"He"?' he said.

He looked around. 'There's still so much to be said,' he said. 'Susannah, when you vanished I was afraid you'd been hurt. Killed even,' he said.

'Yes, well – I'm sorry about that,' she said. After a first moment of being flustered, her self-control reasserted itself. 'Things took an unexpected turn. It was most ... *unfortunate*. Inconvenient for everyone.'

'I'll say,' he agreed, softly. 'You were lucky in a way. You left the apartment just moments before a murder took place there.'

'So I hear. It must have been a shock for you. As I say ...' the words seemed hard to get out for her. 'I'm very sorry.'

'Selling well?' he asked, indicating the six copies of her book and the homemade A4 poster beside them. The poster said: SUSANNAH MOSES' NOMETIC SCIENCE: THE BOOK THE MAINSTREAM MEDIA DON'T WANT YOU TO READ.

She eyed him coldly.

'It's finding a readership,' she said. 'I'm doing the rounds on a lot of podcasts.'

Oh, Richard knew those podcasts. The anti-vax podcasts, the ones about contrails and 5G towers controlling our thoughts. There was a large community to be found there, for sure ...

'I'll buy a copy,' he said, dropping some notes on the table. She rapidly scribbled in the flyleaf of one and handed it over.

'So, humour me,' he said. 'What happened?'

'I got a call,' she said. 'Almost as soon as you left. From my research assistant. It was a ... a very difficult time for me.'

'He told you something about your book,' speculated Richard. 'Something crucial. The experiment results ...'

She nodded.

'He faked them,' Richard said quietly.

Susannah looked around the bookshop, wary of people listening in. Then gave him a look of private exasperation that proved his theory correct.

'You must have been *furious*,' Richard said. 'You were going to be the new Einstein, the next Darwin ...'

'He said he did it for me. Because he couldn't bear to see my work go to waste. He was in love with me. He would do anything for me ...'

'Including ruin your career!' Richard whispered. He was horrified, despite himself. 'That is grotesque!'

He'd read all the stories about the thousands of copies pulped, the events cancelled, the celebrity denunciations. But after all, Susannah had decided to stick to her guns. Claimed that the results were in fact correct after all, and that she had been the victim of a cover-up. A conspiracy.

'You're not wearing a wire?' she asked, guardedly.

His look of three parts shock mixed with one part scorn, sobered her. 'I'm sorry,' she said, in a voice that somewhat chimed with her old personality. 'I'm paranoid. Maybe it's the company I keep. Anyway, I decided that he hadn't ruined my career at all. I chose not to see it that way.'

Richard looked around the bookshop. He had to move momentarily to make way for someone wearing a tin-foil crown. When he met Susannah's eye again, if he had expected her to be shame-faced he was disappointed.

'Guilt is just not my narrative,' she said. 'And think about it this way. Appearing on *The Late Show* as a guest beside Neil deGrasse Tyson is a heck of a lot more stressful than going on Steve Bannon with Naomi Woods. Now even though I know Nometic Science is a bust, I can still make a damn good living off it …'

'But the guy! The lab technician! You should sue him for millions!' Richard expostulated. 'He ruined your life!'

She just smiled. At that moment an enormously handsome man who resembled a Greek god stepped out from the bookshop stockroom. Putting down a quarter of a tonne of book crates and bushing his golden locks back, he bent to give Susannah a kiss on the forehead.

'You okay, hun?' he asked. 'I've made sushi for us. And when you're done, it's massage time.'

When he'd retired to the back of the shop, Susannah turned back to Richard, with a drugged expression. 'As I say,' she said. 'I choose not to see it that way.'

Richard sincerely wished her well, and left the shop.

Life sure is crazy, he thought, as he walked back towards Times Square. *It always throws you a curveball. And you gotta swing in order to hit that ball. If you don't swing, you can't miss. You don't even know what could come from this life. Life! Time! Sixty Seconds!*

He looked along Fifth Avenue, and let out a long breath.

We're always changing. Alchemy is real, it's part of us. It's happening all the time, if only we have the wit to be aware of it happening within us. We are the transition. We are, all of us, every day, trying to transform ourselves from base metal into gold. From unthinking automatons into real, breathing creatures ...

He was starting to feel that the alternative bookshop and the chicory cold-foam latte had affected his brain patterns when he suddenly caught his breath.

Twenty yards ahead, two giant shapes crossed his path.

He gasped.

He felt a strange tremor of fear and memory at the sight of these two giant people. A tremor that he felt all the way down in his lucky Superman underpants. Striding confidently along the street in New York, the only city that was as big as they were, and where they could pass unnoticed. Just two individuals dressed in custom-made garments fashioned surely from abandoned boat tarpaulins or stage curtains, going about their business.

They were holding hands, smiling into each other's eyes, as they crossed Fifth Avenue. Alive, in love and free, while the traffic screeched its brakes, jack-knifed and collided around them, causing millions of dollars of damage and untold injuries.

Richard blinked, and then they were gone. And he couldn't be sure if they'd ever been there at all.

ABOUT THE AUTHOR

BRUNO VINCENT, writing as Dave Beige, is the author of more than thirty books, including the *Sunday Times* bestsellers *Five on Brexit Island*, *Spare Us!* (a parody of Prince Harry's *Spare*) and *Do Ants Have Arseholes?*, which he co-authored with Jon Butler. A former bookseller and editor, he most recently worked on three Sherlock Holmes pastiche mysteries, including *Sherlock Holmes and the Air Fryer of Doom*. He is available to parody weddings, corporate events, bar mitzvahs, supermarket openings ...